B

VanWest
The Present

Book 2 of VanWest Series

Kenneth Thomas

ken@vanwestbooks.com

FIRST EDITION

British English

www.vanwestbooks.com

KDP ISBN: 979-8-64723036-2
ISBN: 978-1-8-3805617-9

Cover design by Elementi Studio

Contents

Prologue

All VanWest knew while growing up was the 'all-knowing' Universal Council. As a loyal Enforcer, he blindly obeyed every command - however dark and morally corrupt.

Commandment 1. To serve without question the Universal Council
Commandment 2. To work for the progression of man and the Universal
Commandment 3. To destroy all those who defy the Universal Council

After being promoted to Captain, VanWest's world as he knew it was to dramatically change. Injured during his victory at the prestigious Universal Red and Blue Games his unique ability was revealed: a latent psychic sense that allowed him to foresee events. The Universal Council and its leader Dr King, greatly alarmed at seeing his visions via the Schuurman Reporting Monitor (SRM), tasked him with a mission to hunt down the Utopians to prevent them from changing the past. His reward the ultimate dream of many a man, woman and child: to become an Elite.

The Utopians, a renegade sect led by the Universal Council's former Head of Science and genius Dr Isaac VonHelmann dubbed 'Mad Newton', had figured out how to travel back in time. Their goal to prevent major events in the mid-to-late 20th century coming to pass that they blamed for ruining Earth and ending the dream of a utopian world by the new millennia. Their targets the creation of the European Nuclear Research Agency (CERN) and the launch of the Unity node, forming the second part of the world's first

International Space Station (ISS) - both significant leaps forward in scientific collaboration and technological advancement.

This challenging mission reunited him with his childhood friend Iris, the daughter of the Utopian leader. She helped him to learn the dark truth about the Universal Council and that of his own origins: a clone of the last Martian President Van der Westhuizen. Having been killed alongside his fellow Martians hundreds of years ago due to the Council's insatiable thirst for power.

Daring to break into the Universal Council's moon base and the notorious Ward B, disguised as Nurse Rose, Iris came to warn that the Council would use him. This would be the first of a series of pivotal meetings that would not only see VanWest change allegiance to save her as he fell in love, but also instigate the citizen uprising now engulfing Queen Elizabeth and many other Antarctic settlements. His Martian psychic ability has matured too, his visions more regular he is able to foresee most, especially imminent, dangers before they occur.

Following the coordinates given to him by Colonel Cornelius, before his death on the arena's floor, he now seeks a path to Mars to kill Dr King and weaken the Space Army that amasses. Joining him is LeSouris, a *Most Wanted* rebel and Utopian, and Iris, his love. The Colonel warned of the 'evil that resides in there', so too did Dr VonHelmann. VanWest worries what he will uncover on Mars, in the Universal Council's hidden base.

With the uprising on Judgment Day, a furious Dr King leaves to Mars via the SCC-400, joining the Space Army's commander Four-star General Vladimir in preparing the Universal spaceships and Space Soldiers to attack Earth. Commissioner Ming, the Head of the Police, is left behind to suppress the uprisings. His mission: to find the traitor VanWest and inflict as much damage as possible on his enemies. At his disposal is a small detachment of Space Soldiers as he tries to strong-arm the Enforcers to come out of their HQs to help him regain control, clearing a path for Dr King's return.

Meanwhile, Dr VonHelmann and Pretoria, the NEA rebel leader, follow VanWest's advice to try to persuade the Enforcers to join the resistance. With Colonel Cornelius's rally and Captain Alpha's death, it has become common knowledge that the Universal Council plans to replace Enforcer with Space Soldier - cyborgs. Captain Kun-lee could be the key as he owes VanWest 'honour'. VanWest and Barys having rescued him from Pytheas's Labyrinth during the Universal Red and Blue Games. Dr VonHelmann hopes to invoke the Enforcer's Code of Honour on VanWest's behalf. And, by right, obtain an audience with the highest-ranking Enforcers in Antarctica, the remaining Colonels, to get them to join the Earth's Resistance Army (EaRA).

Dr VonHelmann's own Utopian mission to change the past a failure, Utopia as he envisioned impossible to regain, now seeks to restart a new brand of this 'New Beginning' in the present, the year 3000. The addition of the Enforcers to Earth's Resistance (EaR) to recreate a new world under the constructs of Utopianism - *led by him*. Without their support, it may be impossible to defeat, even a weakened, Space Army.

VanWest's best and only means to reach Mars lies in New Jersey's crooked underworld, with an NEA contact called Method A; a warlord and casino owner, she could help procure them passage as a stowaway on a cargo ship bound for the red planet.

The stakes could not be higher: if VanWest and Dr VonHelmann are not successful in their missions, millions stand to be massacred.

Chapter 1 The Gambler's Den

One could call the casinos of New Jersey a 30th-century version of Las Vegas, but it is far less glamourous. Its whole existence represents a paradox in this Universal Council ruled world. It serves both as a playground for the Elites, they frequent these casinos for pleasures banned in Antarctica, and a place to negotiate shipments of Papini, a super drug extracted from a mushroom that only grows in its old subway tunnels.

Papini's value is high as all who consume it gain a stronger resistance to the highly radioactive particles prevalent on Earth as well as in Space. Thus, the Jerseyans live in a status quo, their existence accepted but not spoken of. Protected under the PATH agreement, no Universal Council force can step foot inside its territory, only unarmed Elites are permitted by invitation.

The descendants of the first New York mole people, the Jerseyans have lived underground for close to a millennium with little interference from outsiders. Evolving into their own unique homo sapien species during this time, they not only look different but also have an extraordinary resistance to radioactivity, one that no human possesses. Due to their unusual features, including saggy skin, and their general elusiveness many humans derisively refer to them as 'mutants'.

Having come to know Method A during his many NEA smuggling operations in New Jersey, LeSouris's relationship with this warlord will be critical if the trio of VanWest, Iris and LeSouris are to reach a deal for a smuggling operation to Mars. His secretive relationship with her has been lucrative for both sides: for the NEA resources to operate not only in the Antarctic settlements but also across the solar system, and for Method A more 'moolah', currency needed to hold onto her territory Newark - the westerly 'exit' of the PATH network.

LeSouris's stealthy spacecraft, Hawkeye, has gotten them all to New Jersey but is not equipped for long-distance space travel. Now closer to Gambler's Den, VanWest is keen to understand their next steps, anxious about what they will encounter. Having travelled back in time to 1950s Paris and 1990s Florida, only to arrive back in the year 3000 on Judgment Day, he knows to be wary. The Seductress having played both the Universal Council and Utopians for fools as she plotted a 'New Beginning' for herself. He must watch and try to understand the motives of those he meets.

*****

'What's the plan in New Jersey'? VanWest asks LeSouris.

'To get a better ship for Mars'! Iris half-jokes.

'It is not possible! There no one more sexy than Hawkeye'! LeSouris answers with a smile.

'I understand that, but what's the plan'? VanWest presses for more detail.

'My love, LeSouris will ask Method A to help smuggle us inside a Jerseyan cargo ship, one that transports Papini and other goods to the colonies'.

LeSouris adds, 'It will cost, but no one will see us going to Mars. I promise'.

'This Method A that Pretoria spoke of, she has a ship'?

LeSouris explains further, 'My friend, Method A has very big casino, Gambler's Den. Some say this Method A is underground boss, warlord, but she's nothing more than wheeler-dealer. Trust... She knows people who smuggle, makes them deal to pay off their gambling debts'. He pauses, giving VanWest a wink, 'It's straightforward business transaction'!

'Debts? Gambler's Den'? VanWest asks curiously. He has only ever read about such places - casinos having long been banned in Antarctic's settlements.

LeSouris smiles back as if to say he'll find out soon enough. As Hawkeye starts its descent, a dim light breaks through the grey and acidic clouds. The outline of this once megacity's hollow buildings and rooftops appear, prompting a new question from an anxious VanWest, 'Do we have weapons for this place, surely we can't go in unarmed'?

'NO! No! My friend! Would be stupid! We meet our end', LeSouris responds sharply. Iris nodding in agreement.

Enforcer operations are always meticulously planned, but with New Jersey and Method A there are so many unknowns. VanWest has heard only stories and rumours of New Jersey, a violent and large area stretching the length of its ancient subway network called PATH. However, on first appearance, this place looks a lot less foreboding than Queen Elizabeth. Seemingly unaffected by the chaos that ensued in Antarctica, it is eerily quiet. The Jerseyans living and working deep underground, under the ruins on its surface. Hawkeye aligns with the tallest building as it uncloaks to land on its rooftop.

LeSouris whispers to confirm their arrival, 'My friends, welcome to Newark'.

Upon landing, he instructs all to remain still and silent, pressing his index finger against his lips. Through the shutters, VanWest spots someone small and mysterious approaching, dressed in several layers of greyish rags that help it to blend into the surroundings. Its peculiar face stares back at them, its green eyes centred in near-transparent skin that droops from its cheeks to its neck.

This face is not the feature of a sickly looking human, rather what many refer to as a Jerseyan 'mutant'. Even as an Enforcer, VanWest has never seen one up close, for they only leave the PATH network to transport goods to places such as trading posts and prisoner colonies. Very infrequently do they come to any Antarctic settlement where the Enforcers operate, and this only if there is an urgent delivery for an Elite that cannot be collected elsewhere.

LeSouris once again gestures for them to remain silent as he hastily disembarks to greet this Jerseyan. Iris and VanWest only have to wait a few tense seconds before he returns, now ushering them to follow him out. The Jerseyan waves them all through the rooftop to a stairwell at the other end, where LeSouris pushes open a rusty metal door, with a nameplate *Building Eleven* in its centre. They enter *Level 36* and what marks the start of a long, near-endless spiral staircase.

Breathing heavily in the mustardy air, they soon enough reach the ground floor to find another Jerseyan waiting for them. Also wrapped in grey rags, this one holds a long-sticked stun gun called an Electrozapper. The smell now more pungent, it causes their eyes to itch and water. Gesturing with his weapon, he instructs them to pass through a small gap in the wall better suited to that of a diminutive Jerseyan, which at their tallest reach a height of five feet and four inches, a tight squeeze for the six-foot-two-inches VanWest.

VanWest attempts to ask another question, 'There... '? But, before he can continue, LeSouris cuts him off by grabbing his arm to lead him inside - keen for them to move on. VanWest ducks as LeSouris again instructs to 'stay quiet' and to keep their communications to a minimum, not wanting to draw more attention than needed. News of VanWest's 'heroics' in the Colosseum on Judgment Day likely even here already making news.

They hurry through a long narrow corridor to a small metal door at its end. It hangs on one hinge and creaks as LeSouris pushes it open; only to reveal yet another spiral staircase to descend. As they continue down, the dark and dingy walls slowly begin to illuminate, and a faint sound, music, grows. A record that weirdly repeats one line, 'A little less conversation and a little more action'.

'Ladies and Gentlemen, we are entering Vegas. Thank you very much'! LeSouris whispers and gives them a wink, but his smile is unable to hide his trepidation. Having visited many times before, he knows that the warlords, underworld bosses, are erratic and difficult to negotiate with - Method A no different.

'How quaint... King Elvis is alive and well here'! Iris says.

VanWest returns a puzzled expression. He has never heard of this 'King Elvis' and wonders what she means; is this another warlord? His head pounding, sweat dripping down from his brow, he has that instinctive bad feeling but cannot foresee anything. Leaving him unsure if it is: the music, the mustardy smell, or something worse, mortal danger.

At the bottom of the stairs, they find an illuminated golden arched door, guarded on each side by two stocky bouncers. Both wear oversized black sunglasses that hide their wrinkled faces and are dressed in black suits: like all Jerseyan clothes they are made from mycelium fibres - a fungus extract. They continue to stare straight-ahead as they approach, grinding their pointy, metal-plated teeth.

The bouncers finally speak, their voices squeaky, 'Welcome to the Gambler's Den'! Prompting the door to swing open, they appear to recognise LeSouris immediately, allowing them all to pass through without question.

They are met by a bright light that momentarily forces them to shield their eyes. It takes a few moments to adjust, but as it does, VanWest's anxiousness turns to that of wonderment. Greeting them is a most unusual and alien spectacle: a large cathedral ceiling room that houses a lavishly decorated and vibrant casino. They proceed along a long red carpet that leads to a group of golden tables with green tops: the casino pit.

Hunched over the tables is a mix of Jerseyans and lower Elites, also known as 'the descendants'. Their eyes bloodshot, they nervously count their hologram chips as a giant diamond-encrusted roulette wheel spins round in the centre of the room:

inducing the players to place yet more of their hologram chips on rows of numbers in front.

During his Enforcer academy days on the moon, VanWest learnt about this place as an exercise in 'identifying deplorable people and activities'. One thing is for sure, their addictive behaviour shows, none of the players look up: mesmerised by the wheel. So much so that these lower Elites do not notice that the Universal Council's now *Most Wanted* is standing right across them.

VanWest marvels at the spectacle, for a moment nearly forgetting why they have come. This place is a hedonist's paradise. Surrounding the pit are even more games, mainly electronic slot machines with big pull handles, each crank producing a new combination of symbols. On the tables are what appears to be a variety of alcoholic beverages drunken freely as each smokes a pipe linked to a glass vase, *Shisha Pipe.*

Ding-ding-ding! A player on the slots celebrates as the symbols stop with three numbers in a row: *7-7-7*. The sevens remind him of the tattoo on the wrist of his clone source, the deceased Martian President. A once blocked memory that only returned after inserting into his node Dr VonHelmann's green hexagon-shaped chip.

One of the bouncers appears close behind and taps LeSouris on the arm, pointing him to the stairs and a bar that over leans the pit. VanWest and Iris follow; their heads bowed shuffle discreetly a couple of steps behind. At the top of the stairs, they find a flamboyantly dressed Jerseyan waiting, wearing rounded sunglasses, several golden medallions and a purple blouse. This must be Method A! She is sprawled over a similarly coloured semi-circle sofa. Her flabby and wrinkled face greets them, revealing a mouth full of gold and silver, pointy teeth as she grins. Her importance further demarked by several guards that stand nearby, armed with Electrozappers.

* * * * *

'Mister Sour, where've you been'? The Jerseyan warlord greets him, in a squeakier voice than that of her bouncers, she refers to LeSouris by a nickname.

'Warlord Method A, so glad to meet you again! You are looking very well if I may say so'! LeSouris replies in a friendly and respectful manner.

'Bringing me some trouble again, some land-dwellers... Who's that fine skinned thang? A gift, aye'? Method A looks lustfully at Iris, her eyes scanning down from her smooth lips and along her slender body.

'Hey! Watch it'! VanWest forgets himself and responds indignantly. Reacting to what he perceives as extreme rudeness, unaware that this behaviour is considered quite acceptable in Jerseyan society - even a compliment.

VanWest's anger only serves to garner the attention of Method A's guards, who point their long-sticked stun guns towards him.

'Relax dawg! Come here and chill. Have drag on me'. Fortunately, Method A does not take issue, as LeSouris looks sheepishly at VanWest to accept her offer. Waving her guards away, she presents a pipe filled with a pinkish powder.

'Excuse him, Method A. He meant no disrespect', LeSouris apologises, nudging VanWest to take the pipe and have a puff.

VanWest tentatively takes hold. Having never smoked before, he is unsure how to use it. The scent alone is enough to make him light-headed, his eyes widening, and his body feeling ever so relaxed. LeSouris quickly takes it back and returns it to Method A.

'Method A, we come seeking transport to the colonies and would be grateful for your help', LeSouris requests.

However, Method A's mood visibly changes as she casts her eyes over Iris again, this time more focused. Almost leaping from her sofa, she realises that these are not any normal 'land-dwellers', NEA rebels that LeSouris usually asks to help smuggle.

She looks angrily at LeSouris and scolds him, 'No play me, Sour! I know this dawg and chick. Them two on news wire all time. You know this brings heat on my casino'!

Le Souris struggles to reply, stuttering, 'Apol-apologies, Method A. We work many years together. I can pay. I have...'

'We have come to do a deal', Iris interjects in an authoritative tone, trying to take control of the negotiation and situation. Only angering Method A further.

'Zip it! You cause me lot of problems coming here, better you stay in Queenie, be good thang'. Looking back at LeSouris, 'Sour, this too big, there's not enough moolah... Too much heat'! An increasingly vexed Method A takes off her sunglasses and throws them onto the black table, revealing her small green and scowling eyes, as her guards step forward with their Electrozappers.

LeSouris signals to Iris to let him continue, discreetly patting her on the back, and removes a large pink gem from his pocket - a precious diamond. This moolah is worth at least 10,000 crates of Papini, far higher than the usual price to smuggle anyone to Mars. But, then again, these aren't the usual stowaways - they are the instigators of the citizen's uprising.

VanWest recognises this gem. It looks remarkably like the one stolen from the Hubert collection, the Elite business family and owners of many brands such as Demron and InsectnOut. Indeed, he was there when it was taken during a failed NEA assassination attempt in his first tour as an Enforcer when he rescued their family head. A reminder that not so long ago LeSouris and him were on opposite sides - enemies.

Rare gems, particularly pink diamonds, remain one of the most prized commodities throughout the last millennium, even after mining operations increased production across the solar system their value has not diminished. The Jerseyan warlords, at least Method A, seem to be as avid collectors of these decorative and rare gems as the Elites.

Method A takes the diamond from his hand, 'Sour, you put me in sticky situation, but I'm fair A. I tell you all options, best I do for old time sake, we play Red and Black. You lose I give Enforcer dawg to Council and keep that fine skinned thang'.

'No way! Pay only, Method A'! LeSouris refuses to gamble their lives in a game of roulette.

Method A continues, 'You win they go. I only take your moolah for ship to Mars. Fair deal'. Method A's big grin returning, she shows off all her pointy gold and silver teeth. It's very much a win-win deal for her, as the saying goes 'the house always wins'.

'Rotten deal'! Iris shouts angrily and lurches belligerently at Method A to give her a punch. Still slightly spaced out, VanWest just about manages to pull her back before she can get close. Saving them all from getting struck by an Electrozapper. Iris adds, 'Call me fine thang again, I'll slit your throat, you low-life'!

Method A laughs, 'Me like lively ones', amused by her reaction. But, in a more serious tone, she instructs LeSouris to take the gamble, 'Best deal. Only deal'.

Her sunglasses fall to the floor as the black table starts to rotate. Slowly transforming into a shiny golden wheel that spins hypnotically. Next, 30 numbers project upwards from its rim, the evens in black and the odds in red, a lone green for zero.

'Sour, I give you red. I give fair odds... maybe you lucky, aye', Method A passes to LeSouris a hologram ball to drop inside.

Still holding Iris's arm, VanWest looks around for an escape route, but every exit is guarded. Furthermore, neither he nor Iris are armed. LeSouris indeed has only one choice, either he plays this game or risks them all being zapped. The game is not quite as 'fair' as Method A presents, it is stacked in favour of the house and not 50-50. For if the ball lands on either black or the lone green they will lose.

But VanWest's walk through the casino pit has triggered an idea. Remembering how focused the gamblers were, he thinks that the roulette game and its bouncing ball could provide a useful distraction; enough time for him to make a run at Method A and to catch her in a headlock before her guards can react. The threat of him snapping her neck could, in turn, give them much more favourable odds of getting them all out and to Mars.

With time not on their side, VanWest releases Iris's arm with a wink, to signal a plan is afoot and pushes a nervous-looking LeSouris forward to take the gamble. At the same time, discreetly stepping behind him and one step closer to Method A. LeSouris shakes his head but submits and drops the hologram ball into the roulette wheel, allowing VanWest to take another small step forward.

The game commences as the ball hits the rim and bounces into the centre, bouncing several times more across, from black to red and back again, as the wheel starts to slow. Disguised as that of interest in the game, VanWest shifts forward once more. Method A and her guards are indeed too distracted to notice, too eager to find out the result.

The ball jumps up one last time, skipping just past a black slot as it comes to a stop on number *15*, red. But VanWest does not wait to see if Method A will hold true to her word and leaps at her before the guards can react. In a split-second places her flabby neck inside a headlock as they crash down onto the floor. Her guards surround them, unsure how to react - if they shoot they risk hitting her.

Method A though is strangely relaxed, quite amused and still grinning. She mouths the words, 'Thought you chill dawg, look you won... Keep fine skinned thang, aye'!

As she speaks, a vision flashes across VanWest's mind, that of Space Soldiers racing into the casino pit. Knowing the PATH agreement, VanWest is shocked to foresee this grave violation! Such is their desire to stop him that the Universal Council is willing to bring the chaos in Antarctica to New Jersey. Loosening his grip, VanWest pulls Method A back to her feet as she signals for her guards to stand down.

VanWest looks straight into her small, green eyes and in a low voice shares his ominous warning, 'Method A, there... Space Soldiers come'.

Method A's grin instantly evaporates, she knows he is serious as she looks over at her Jerseyan guards, their Electrozappers point now over at the red carpet and entrance to Gambler's Den. The ground slightly vibrates.

VanWest leans over, whispering in her ear, 'Dr King and the Space Army is amassing over Mars. These Soldiers are just the first, more will come. New Jersey will share the same fate as Antarctica. Remember that'. A not so subtle urging for her to join them in Earth's resistance.

Staying true to her deal, a visibly shocked Method A instructs, 'Land-dwellers, I have moolah... Get out, take path behind that room over there. My dawg Gs will help ye'!

Seeing the players, croupiers and servers starting to flee the casino pit, a bemused LeSouris asks, 'What's happening'?

'Run'! Method A shouts.

'Roaching run'! VanWest repeats before turning and running down the stairs, the ground vibrates more and the lights flicker, just like on Ward B when the Colonel arrived - a spaceship is close, and Space Soldiers are marching. Iris and LeSouris look at each other and quickly follow. The vibrations only intensifying; it's as if the place is being struck by an earthquake. The slot machines, roulette and blackjack tables come crashing down, as more of Method A's guards race in to take up positions by the entrance.

As they reach a small room, VanWest glances back at the casino pit - catching a glimpse of the near cyclops-eyed Commissioner Ming, in his black peaked cap, walking through the golden arched entrance. As foreseen, he's accompanied by several Space Soldiers, an egregious violation of the PATH agreement.

Chapter 2 A Crate Full of Papini

LeSouris knows the way from here and reveals a well-hidden escape route as he lifts up a loose brick, causing a section of the wall to jut forward and slide open. In front lies a narrow, darkly lit tunnel, the opening even lower than that on the way to Gambler's Den. LeSouris enters first, crawling on all fours. Iris and VanWest follow - the wall shifting back into place after they pass. The mustardy smell grows ranker; they must be getting closer to the Papini crop and to the subway tunnels.

The ground continues to shake, causing the metal beams above to vibrate and dust to cover them. With Commissioner Ming and the Space Soldiers entering the casino, they move as fast as possible to get away and soon reach what appears to be a ventilation shaft: its metal rusty and badly corroded. A dim light reveals another larger tunnel below; the floor lined with wooden sleepers connected by iron. Without pausing, LeSouris slides down. Iris does her best to follow but lands awkwardly - fortunate to only receive a small cut on her knee as she stumbles forward.

VanWest follows behind, landing beside he helps her up and to wipe away the dust. Giving her a gentle and reassuring kiss on her head as he does so. These are rail tracks; its good condition indicating that they are still in use. The age of the tunnels gives VanWest the uneasy feeling that he has travelled back in time once again but quickly realises that they have arrived inside New Jersey's subway system: the PATH network that connects New Jersey to New York. More than a thousand years old, it was originally built when these states were part of the now-dissolved union called the United States of America.

As the Earth's surface became hotter and less habitable, its overground sections were covered by a thick reinforced concrete roof, subsequently buried under tons of sand and rubble. Protected from the radioactive and toxic air, it evolved from a subway network into a dwelling and then settlement in its own right. The mole people its earliest inhabitants, many escaping the pressures of society, such as paying taxes and rent. It soon attracted those from all walks of life, who came to make this their home, from as far away as Canada and Mexico. These the few that refused to migrate to the cooler Antarctic region, ruled by the Oligarchs, later to become known as the Elites.

VanWest marvels as he looks up at the sloped walls and concave ceiling, it is filled with thousands upon thousands of small mushrooms, Papini. The source of the mustardy smell, they are white in colour and take various shapes, sprouting out of cracks between the bricks. Ultra-violet light bulbs that dangle every dozen yards serve as their only source of light. It's incredible how many mushrooms grow here, the crop spreading for miles and miles along the tracks.

Hush! Suddenly, two large creatures with twelve eyes and eight legs scurry out to greet them. Curling over their back is an intimidating segmented tail, which curves over and points forward towards them, at its end a stinger. If not threatening enough, each carries enormous claws on their front pair of legs, a single pinch of which would surely snap them in half. VanWest gasps, having dealt with gigantic spiders and wild roaches before, he instinctively grabs a large fallen brick from the floor, ready to fight them off. But to his astonishment, LeSouris laughs and walks over to the creatures. One is slightly larger than the other. It carries on its back several mini versions of itself - its babies.

LeSouris gives each a pat and says, 'My friends, let me introduce Ken and Barbie! Are they not the cutest daddy, mommy you have ever seen'? And gives them another stroke on their horned heads.

Iris seems to know what they are and says, 'King scorpions'?

LeSouris answers, 'Yes! They're good companions, ever so cuddly, these two my personal favourites. Yes you are, yes you are'. He speaks to them as if they were his pets.

King scorpions are one of the few creatures able to survive radiation poisoning, living cordially alongside the Jerseyans, they protect the Papini crop and rail tracks. *Screech!* A large metal container comes rolling towards them. Breaking heavily, it grinds to a halt only a few steps away.

LeSouris gives them a reassuring wink and taps its side, instructing, 'My friends, transport... trust'! Iris looks at VanWest, signalling for him to get in. They need to get going, the ground even this far below the surface is vibrating.

Once inside, the cart automatically rolls forward for a few meters before accelerating rapidly. Before they know it, VanWest and Iris find themselves climbing up towards an illuminated red sign, its letters reading *WARNING STEEP DESCENT*. The tracks look to be coming to an end!

Seeing LeSouris bracing himself by holding onto the side and bowing his head, Iris and VanWest promptly do the same. The cart quickly passing by the sign, they are sent in a near-vertical freefall - *whoosh*, neither Iris nor VanWest sure what is happening and where they're heading. The cart sways from side to side but somehow sticks to the tracks; fortunately, it soon begins to level once again. However, this white-knuckle ride is not quite over, about 100 yards ahead is a long line of mining carts. Going so fast, it looks like they are going to collide. Sparks fly all around as LeSouris brakes heavily - *screech,* forcefully pulling a lever backwards. VanWest checks if Iris is ok, her eyes remaining shut, she can't bear to look as she continues to hold on tightly.

To his relief the cart finally slows down, coming to a thudding stop, a small shunt connects it to the cart in front, throwing them slightly forwards - *clink*. LeSouris looks unfazed, seemingly quite accustomed to this method of transport - he must have done this ride a few times before.

LeSouris points further down the tunnel, instructing them to get out and continue on foot, 'This way'!

Helping each other out of the cart, they hurry through the dim light until LeSouris finally stops. There's an unmarked door, so hard to spot it blends in with the Papini and bricks. As LeSouris pushes it open, a waft of hot steam blows into their faces, so thick it partially obscures what appears to be a very long and slender object inside, on closer inspection a Jerseyan cargo ship. It stands tall in the middle of a silo with a high-pitched ceiling, not too dissimilar in size to the hangar VanWest saw in Homestead Airport, in 1998 Florida.

Following LeSouris and Iris inside, VanWest is startled to find a small Jerseyan in a black helmet and visor staring up at them, 'Hey'!

The Jerseyan greets LeSouris, 'Hey, Mister Sour! Brought me some land peeps'?

'Oh yes, good to see you, Gs. Been a long time, my friend'! LeSouris answers with a smile, the two having met on previous smuggling operations.

'Get your bruva and sista in cargo hold, inside blue crate... Papini. Gotta be quick and quiet', Gs instructs.

'What? Till Mars'? Iris interrupts, looking unimpressed.

'Is it safe'? VanWest asks more pertinently.

'This is how one smuggles'! LeSouris replies with a shrug of his shoulders.

'Can we trust him'? VanWest looks pointedly at LeSouris, this time asking more directly. Worried that Gs could sell them out, much as Method A threatened to do so earlier.

LeSouris shrugs his shoulders again as if to say that it's not like they have a choice, 'My friend, Method A let us "land-dwellers" go, so I say trust... She is woman of her word, her Jerseyans are loyal. I travelled in crates before, it works... A tried and tested method'.

Gs interjects, looking at each in turn, 'Sour, bruva, sista, you can trust me. I always fulfil deals, especially for my boss, Method A'! Not yet quite realising who he has been asked to smuggle.

With the Commissioner's arrival, there only hope lies with a quick escape on Gs's cargo ship, there is no time to discuss further. They need to go! VanWest nods and double-checks the coordinates of this Universal Council base on Mars, activating Colonel Cornelius's red diamond chip into his node. The base is located in Arcadia MC-03, close to a volcano in Alba Mons. There he expects to find not only Dr King but also his Head of Science, Dr Minus Schuurman. The dying Colonel Cornelius giving him the troubling warning to 'beware' of himself. It pains him to think what 'evil' he will encounter - that he has yet to realise.

He leans down, asking Gs, 'Can you get us to MC-03, Arcadia'?

Gs rolls his small green eyes, protesting, 'Cargo ship destined for different zone. Looksie suspicious if go there. No good'!

Knowing the importance of getting there, LeSouris unfolds his Moggleapp tablet, 'I see small colony and trading post nearby... Arcadia Plains. Gs, my friend, you know of this place'?

Gs sighs and rechecks his schedule, before replying, 'You mess up my plans'.

'My friend, small detour, no'?

'Tell me, why there'? Gs asks curiously.

VanWest doesn't want to reveal the real reason and thus opts to tell him a lie, 'Oh... Got to escape the chaos in Antarctica, need a hideout... this place is rarely visited'.

At that moment Gs realises who he is, gulping, 'Ah, you that Captain dawg'!

Understanding their urgency to get as far away as possible, he agrees, 'I get you to Arcadia Plains. I make an order for my contact there, Sista Cees'.

'Thanks', Iris replies.

'Thank Method A, pay all my spinning wheel debts', Gs says with a big grin, showing his rotten, pointy teeth.

Not plated in metal, let alone silver and gold, his teeth are a sign of his need for moolah. It's not only the Elites that are avid gamblers in New Jersey but so too its locals. Like many other Jerseyans, Gs has high gambling debts. So high in fact that he's even willing to take the Universal Council's *Most Wanted* on a dangerous smuggling operation to Mars to pay it off.

Wah-wah! Gs grin quickly disappears, replaced by a look of dread as a red-light flashes and a siren sounds: Newark has gone into full alert and lockdown. Gs ushers them inside the ship's hold, looking more nervous by the second as sweat drips down his wrinkled face.

'What the... break PATH agreement'! Gs mutters in astonishment.

With this siren, they realise Commissioner Ming's incursion spreads from Gambler's Den and encompasses all of Newark - the skies will soon be in lockdown. Even with the chaos engulfing Antarctica, the Commissioner dares to bring about a confrontation with the Jerseyans. There must be more happening than simply capturing VanWest.

After the citizens' uprising, the Universal Council has placed, in effect, the whole of Earth in lockdown. The Commissioner comes to New Jersey to exert control with the help of a small contingent of Space Soldiers stationed close to Earth, he seeks to pave the way for Dr King's vengeful return with an armada of spaceships. The Commissioner's vanguard will no doubt cause as much destruction and bloodshed as possible, making the trio's mission to find and kill Dr King even more urgent.

Like with Hawkeye, this ship doesn't have a transporter, they clamber in through the cargo hold's wide doors. Gs wastes no time, giving each a satchel bag containing a large blue pill and gestures for each to swallow it whole and then lay down in a crate filled with bags of Papini powder. Bags likely destined for a prisoner colony. The pill induces a catatonic sleep-like state, providing a useful aid for smuggling as it lowers the heart rate. Combined with the strong muster of Papini, it masks heat signatures and helps avoid detection.

Gs says, 'Ship gotta move slowly to act normal. Be 1 day, 2 days travel. Take pill, I meet you on other side'.

LeSouris does not hesitate to swallow. However, VanWest and Iris seek reassurance, given the scene in the casino earlier, they are understandably distrusting. But with the red-light flashing, there is no time to discuss.

LeSouris urges, 'My friends, take it. Trust in Utopia'!

Before swallowing, Iris and VanWest exchange a warm embrace and kiss, and then step inside their crates to lay down in the middle of the bags as instructed.

VanWest tries to stay positive, and not show too much his concern, 'My sweet, I'll see you on the other side. Like I said in Florida, in the past, we will build a wonderful new future together'.

Iris does the same, 'My love, I trust we will have a bright future. We must stay strong. Sleep well, and let us bless our voyage to Mars with a few words of hope'.

The effect of the sleeping pill quickly takes hold as Iris recites her favourite Emily Dickinson poem, the same one she started back in Ward B, inside the Asclepius medical complex. Her voice soothing:

"Hope" is the thing with feathers -
That perches in the soul -
And sings the tune without the words -
And never stops - at all -

And sweetest - in the Gale -
And sore must be the storm -
That could abash the little Bird
That kept so many warm -

I've heard it in the chilliest land -
And on the strangest Sea -
Yet - never - in Extremity,
It asked a crumb - of me.

As Gs places the lids back on top of the crates, the engines of the ship ignite, and the roof of the silo slides open. VanWest tries to call out as all goes dark, but finds himself no longer laying inside the crate. Rather, he stands in front of a man in a white jumpsuit that looks remarkably like himself, only older and greyer. On the man's wrist is a tattoo, 777. He tries to approach, only for an intense green light to push him back. This is not an older version of himself, rather as Dr VonHelmann showed him in his interface as a child, his clone source, the Martian President Van der Westhuizen.

The green light widens and engulfs the man, fragmenting him into a thousand little pieces as an altogether different scene emerges, a street lined with bright white capsule buildings, located in-between trees and flowers. It looks wondrous and surreal, nearly as green as the Everglades of 1998 Florida.

Turning his head slightly, he catches the last glimmers of the light in the distance. Towering over a square decorated with dark blue stones stands a prominent building different from the rest, built of decorative red brick. On its pointy coned shaped roof, a large cross rises and something entirely unexpected too, a large golden *U*. The first the symbol of Christianity, the other that of Utopianism. It appears to be a church and a place where both religions intertwine. A paradox in itself, one a religion that no longer exists in the Antarctic settlements, the other only meant to have come into existence in recent times. Here, they overlap, they are linked to one another.

He feels strangely compelled to walk towards the red brick building before the last glimmers of light disappear. But when he tries to approach, he finds that he cannot control his movements. Stumbling forward, he finds himself in front of the church. He looks up to see a little girl with dark green eyes, in her small hands she clutches an orange-yellow stone. Looking at him lovingly, like a daughter does to her father, she also looks terrified - a lone tear rolls down her cheek.

He bends down to give her a kiss on the cheek, only for a blast to knock them both to the ground. Now, he lies on the floor, inside the church, holding her limp and lifeless body in his arms, her eyes glazed over and blank. VanWest feels a cold chill running down his spine, overwhelmed by grief and horror. He feels utterly helpless - unable to move.

As he stares mournfully into her eyes, the scene fragments and the green plants turn to ash; the capsule pods are charred and twisted. He realises he is watching a painful memory not quite his own. There's a voice calling to him, 'wake up'. It repeats again. The scene changes once more, with him trying to shift a heavy slab back over a hole, just about fitting it into place before another blast of light disintegrates everything.

Chapter 3 There is Honour Among Enforcers

Dr VonHelmann arrives in Mid-City, Queen Elizabeth, along with Pretoria, the settlement's NEA rebel leader. His wounds have been mostly healed whilst in the hovercar, but his 700-year-old body remains very fragile. NEA Intel confirms that Captain Kun-lee has indeed retreated inside the Enforcer HQ, as have most of his fellow Enforcers, now debating their next steps after Colonel Cornelius's rallying cry and subsequent death at the hands of Dr King on Judgment Day.

Hoping to broker a deal, Pretoria has instructed his fellow NEA rebels to avoid any engagement with the Enforcers; focusing their firepower instead on the patrol androids, Quadrotors and anything else machine-like. Having saved Captain Kun-lee during the Universal Games, VanWest has advised Dr VonHelmann to invoke the Code of Honour on his behalf to open talks between NEA and Enforcer. The Enforcers live and die by the Spartan system: one that emphasises discipline, endurance and duty. Honour between them transcends rank and must be respected. His call must be heard.

Never has there been a greater opportunity, the Colonel's death another confirmation that the Space Soldiers' role is expanding. With their own role already reduced to that of patrolling larger Antarctic settlements, it would not take much to replace them entirely. Bringing with it an even more oppressive rule over the citizens - treated by the cold hand of the Soldier, their lives will become as grim as those in the prisoner colonies.

The population already much smaller compared to the start of the third millennium, the only real need for citizens by the Universal Council is as a source of cheap labour. In many respects, they have become a more disposable asset than cyborgs and machines. The second commandment and Enforcer's motto: to *work for the progression of man and the Universal Council*, only ever applied to the Elites.

Unbeknownst to Dr VonHelmann and Pretoria is that with Colonel Cornelius's death and Commissioner Ming's incursion in New Jersey, the academy's professor Master Jiang has arrived to oversee operations in the capital, tasked with mobilising the Enforcers into 'subduing' the populace. This one-time Elite guard has been close to the Universal Council's leadership for hundreds of years. He even partnered with Dr VonHelmann, when was still Head of Science, to test many of his inventions and recommend Enforcers for his experiments. Foremost a Universal Council loyalist and one of Dr King's most trusted henchmen, he will obstruct any peace talks.

Between the smouldering buildings, Dr VonHelmann and Pretoria can see the Enforcer HQ, surrounded and protected by its own forcefield. With no other way to enter, Dr VonHelmann decides on the brazen move of simply walking up to the perimeter and requesting to speak to Captain Kun-lee. His reasoning that with Earth's insurrection growing, the Enforcers are at a disadvantage and don't want to attract any attention, well at least not yet. With the Space Army amassing, there's no time to dither. For Earth's Resistance Army (EaRA) to succeed, he needs the wavering Enforcers on his side.

Dr VonHelmann tells Pretoria, 'Dear friend, I must go to the forcefield. There, I will ask for this Captain Kun-lee'.

'Me make there too, talk for NEA', Pretoria replies firmly, as keen to strike a deal. 'NEA, Enforcer make peace. Too much death already'.

'Very well, let us trust and go together'! Upon which Dr VonHelmann embraces him by the hand and elbow.

*****

Both unarmed, Pretoria helps a frail Dr VonHelmann to the outer perimeter of the HQ, its forcefield around 100 yards away. Fortunately, the way there is relatively calm, and the black smoke keeps them hidden from the occasional patrol android and Quadrotor that whizzes overhead. Standing guard in this section are four heavily armed Enforcers, having already zoomed in on them, they look shocked to identify the doctor, or 'Mad Newton' as they have come to know him. Unsure how to react and expecting a trap, they move cautiously forward to intercept by assuming a defensive square formation. As they do so, an Enforcer watchtower swings around to point a heavy mounted Plasma blaster.

'Halt'! One yells, his plasma rifle pointing at their heads, and its orange light blinding.

Waaahhhh! A siren follows. Its screech forcing them to their knees as they instinctively try to cover their ears. Before Dr VonHelmann can even ask to see Captain Kun-lee, the lead Enforcer throws on each an Electrolock, imprisoning them and leaving them spasming and unable to talk. Ranked a sergeant, Chang's primary task is to guard the base, and he's not interested in talking. The other Enforcers stand guard, expecting other 'hostiles' to come next as the Sergeant drags his captives to the inner perimeter of the base, where more Enforcers wait on full alert.

Pretoria and Dr VonHelmann's bodies continue to spasm as they are dragged through a narrow door and taken to separate holding cells. Similar in design to those of the Interrogator on the SCC-400, the cells are square and surrounded by red pulsating laser bars. Thrown inside, their bodies hit the concrete floor with a loud thud. Out of the dozens of cells lining the cold corridor, theirs are the only ones occupied: the Enforcers clearly not keen to hold any citizen or rebel for fear of reprisal - Dr VonHelmann's incarceration bringing much tension to an HQ seeking to keep a low profile as they decide on their next steps.

Having hoped to call on Captain Kun-lee at the perimeter, to invoke the Code of Honour all they can do now is wait. Free of the Electrolock they sit with their legs crossed, trying to remain as calm as possible. Mentally preparing themselves for whatever may come next. It takes several long hours before Sergeant Chang returns, this time flanked by an anxious-looking Captain Dell. With his Electrolock at the ready once again, it looks like they are to be moved. Pretoria looks over at Dr VonHelmann, mouthing 'make strong' as the pulsating red bars fade.

Dr VonHelmann reacts quicker this time, taking this opportunity to shout at them, his voice hoarse, 'Captain Kun-lee, I call on the Code of Honour on behalf of Captain VanWest'!

But it falls on deaf ears, Sergeant Chang restrains him once again in an Electrolock, and he spasms terribly. They do the same to Pretoria, taking them both to the elevator and up to the command deck of the HQ. Its panoramic views showing the whole capital blanketed in black smoke and most of its buildings destroyed. Whilst relieved to find a nervous-looking Captain Kun-lee standing in the middle of the room, they are more startled to find Master Jiang there too. His black eyes scowling at them both.

The communication station's holoscreen brings two of the highest-ranking Enforcers into the room: Colonel Mason of ColaBeers and Colonel Mathieu of Ellsworth. Mercifully, Master Jiang takes the decision to release them from the Electrolocks, leaving them on their knees and Captain Dell's plasma rifle trained on them.

Captain Dell announces, 'Sergeant Chang captured Mad Newton and a helper at the perimeter'. Prompting the NEA leader to reply, in an indignant voice, 'My name, PRETORIA'!

Master Jiang looks amused and replies, 'Pretoria! Oh my, we thought you were long dead'. Adding sarcastically, 'Wow, the NEA leader has come to welcome me to Queen Elizabeth, what a treat! To what do I owe the pleasure'?

'You cannot make me dead'! Pretoria says proudly.

'Well, that's not so true anymore, is it'? Master Jiang replies with a wry smile, causing Captain Dell and Sergeant Chang to snigger. However, Captain Kun-lee remains silent, watching unamused. This small act of insubordination does not go unnoticed by Master Jiang, who gives him a derisory look. The correct behaviour is to fawn over their masters, laugh at their jokes. But, after the killings in the Colosseum on Judgment Day, Kun-lee does not want to see anyone else being executed.

He's not alone, Colonel Mathieu watching via the holoscreen interjects and asks both captives a question, 'Do you come in peace'?

'Silence! Colonel Mathieu you would be wise to remember the commandments and your command line', Master Jiang replies angrily, for he is the highest-ranked of all and he chooses who can speak.

Being nearly mockingly submissive, Colonel Mathieu replies with a small bow, 'Apologies Master Jiang, may I beg your permission to speak'.

Observing Colonel Mathieu willingness to listen, Dr VonHelmann addresses him directly, 'Colonel, we call the Code of Honour... For VanWest saved Captain Kun-lee at the Universal Games'.

Ha-ha! This time only Master Jiang laughs. Captain Kun-lee looks over at the Colonels expectantly, wanting them to reply on his behalf. This is 'Honour', it must be respected. It cannot be overruled, especially if it is not deemed to violate the Universal Council's commandments.

This prompts Colonel Mathieu to reply, in open defiance of Master Jiang, he feels compelled to listen to this request, 'Is this true, is there honour'?

Master Jiang hectors again, 'Silence! Your insubordination smacks of treason. There IS no honour reserved for this deviant. His execution will soon be broadcasted, made an example of. All those who defy the Universal Council will be destroyed'!

Captain Kun-lee summons the courage to speak up, he cannot standby any longer, 'Master Jiang, honour is at stake. Without it, we are nothing'.

Sensing that he is losing control, Master Jiang reacts aggressively and grabs Kun-lee's throat, 'Are you trying to tell me, you to be a deviant and traitor like the Colonel and VanWest'? And then signals for Captain Dell to turn his rifle on Kun-lee.

'Stop'! Dr VonHelmann tries to bring calm, 'Captain VanWest saved his life in the Universal Games, the favour must be returned. Master Jiang... we merely ask to talk freely without thy retribution'.

Colonel Mathieu agrees, 'There is enough chaos out there, we don't need it in here. Let's talk... no commandment is defied by talking'.

Captain Dell stares at both in utter confusion, unsure what to do and who to obey, his rifle trembling. Captain Kun-lee bravely repeats, 'Master... there IS honour'.

An incensed Master Jiang commands, 'Captain, do OBEY your master'!

A communication interrupts the tense stand-off, Commissioner Ming's 4D hologram appearing in front. Dr VonHelmann and Pretoria decide it best to not speak and look to the floor, heads bowed. Having heard of their capture, he looks pleased, 'Congratulations on capturing Mad Newton, be sure to execute him promptly, be sure to broadcast it to all'!

Wanting to look in control, Master Jiang opts not to mention to their argument and stand-off, in particular Colonel Mathieu's defiance, 'Of course. We shall do so'!

Commissioner Ming tone though becomes more foreboding, 'Be sure to do so with haste. Enforcers as re-affirmation of the commandments, the progression of man and the Universal, MUST retake the streets and pave the way for the return of the Space Soldiers. They will hold the settlements and prevent more insurrections'.

'They will hold the settlements' is not a careless slip, rather it's an open declaration that the role of the Space Soldiers is expanding. The Commissioner continues, 'Be sure to remember who you serve! Do not disgrace the Universal Council further, like those weak-minded Enforcers', referring to Colonel Cornelius and Captain VanWest.

In a hurry to return to his own mission, the incursion into New Jersey, the communication ends abruptly.

With the room distracted and only Sergeant Chang's rifle trained on him, Pretoria deems it best to act and not wait for the discussion to resume. He throws one of his large fists back, knocking the Sergeant's plasma rifle to the floor and the other straight into Captain Dell's jaw before he can turn. Dr VonHelmann drops his frail body over the Sergeant's rifle, the best he can do to help as Pretoria delivers another hard fist into Dell's face, knocking him onto his backside.

Somewhat ironically, having just accused Captain Kun-lee of being a deviant and traitor, Master Jiang commands him now to engage Pretoria, 'Shoot! Shoot'! Having spent the last 80 years as a professor, he has become careless and carries no weapon.

With Master's Jiang unable to punish them, an emboldened Kun-lee raises his voice, 'There is honour among us, and I will answer the Code of Honour between the Enforcer VanWest and myself. NEA and Enforcer will speak without fear of retribution. To discuss an END to hostilities'.

'Hear, hear', Colonel Mathieu agrees. However, Colonel Mason remains silent, all the time watching in a calculating manner. He is neither a winner of the Games nor a decorated hero, his background similar to that of Master Jiang, an Elite guard and henchman of Dr King.

Master Jiang tone weakens but he continues to menace, 'The Universal Council is all-knowing and your master. VanWest has no honour, this deviant is no longer an Enforcer, this Code of Honour does not apply. This is final'!

Colonel Mathieu replies sharply, 'The Code of Honour stands no matter what'!

'Colonel, you continue to display deviant behaviour... like Colonel Cornelius'!

Hitting a nerve it prompts Colonel Mathieu to ask a direct question about the Enforcers' future, 'With respect, Dr King killed the Colonel. You heard the Commissioner, are we all not next? Tell us the truth'!

Master Jiang hesitates and then tries to deflect the question, 'Your... affection for the deviant Colonel poisons your mind. You forget he killed an Enforcer, Captain Alpha'.

Colonel Mathieu says, 'Alpha was a cyborg, a Space Soldier. Despite his selfish, unbrotherly behaviour, the Universal Council promoted him, designating him a leader at every opportunity. He was a test to replace us, correct'?

'SILENCE'! Master Jiang commands.

Colonel Mathieu presses, 'Admit it! Captain Alpha is the future, cyborgs the new Enforcers, the academy gone'!

Colonel Mathieu has been an Enforcer, come Elite, for over 100 years - his life artificially prolonged. His relationship with Colonel Cornelius longstanding, in the Universal Games of 2995 it was he who coached him to victory, just as the Colonel did for Captain VanWest five years later. They were most fond of each other. He too knows the history of the Space Soldiers, they were once like the Enforcers are now.

At first enhanced with bionics, slowly over time, they became more machine than human - the commander of the Space Army, Four-star General Vladimir, the last not to be a cyborg. Everyone else is so, including Lt. Colonel Omega and Major Chromes. With no Spartan mantra of treating each other as equals, they only care about serving the Universal Council, doing whatever their master requests: not tied by any Code of Honour.

Colonel Mathieu cannot take the Council's lies any longer, he goes a step further than VanWest's and Dr VonHelmann's request by giving his support to the Enforcers to decide their own futures, 'I grant all the Enforcers a vote, a free vote on a ceasefire with the NEA and the beginning of talks on a new order'.

Flabbergasted Master Jiang forbids it, 'Colonel! A vote? You defy the sacred commandments! Defy the will and power of the Universal Council! The Commissioner will hear of this, you will be executed. This will not go ahead under my watch'.

Looking at the other Enforcers, Colonel Mathieu asks, 'Who else here is a traitor'?

Having stayed quiet, Colonel Mason makes his position clear, 'The Enforcers of ColaBeers stand to serve our masters, the Universal Council. We do not defy'.

With the mining settlement of ColaBeers not under seize, a sad consequence of Captain VanWest's success in wiping the NEA out during his second tour, he chooses to stay loyal to Dr King's even if this means the end of his own Enforcers.

Chapter 4 A Free Vote

There has been no democracy on Earth for centuries, the Enforcers always order takers, serving their masters *-for the progression of man and the Universal.* Master Jiang knows a vote, any talks with the enemy for that matter, is not a proposal Dr King and the Universal Council would ever accept.

Dr VonHelmann looks straight at Master Jiang, hoping he can still convince him to switch allegiance, 'The Council's authority is no more. They are the past. Master Jiang, let thyself be part of the New Beginning. Trust in a future free of cyborgs and evil machines'.

'Mad Newton... I'm not so easy to brainwash. I know you seek power, your motive not cohesion and progress', Master Jiang retorts angrily.

Dr VonHelmann continues, 'You and I are not so different. Tell me thy teachings, they are founded in kung fu are they not? Are these teachings intended for machines'?

'YOU and I are nothing alike'!

Pretoria adds his voice, 'Rebel, Utopian, citizens make great force around HQ, in every settlement but ColaBeers. Enforcer can join next. Together, we can make Earth strong. Stop the Council's Space Army'.

Still, Master Jiang resists, dismissing Pretoria's words he looks straight at Dr VonHelmann and says, 'Don't use the same trickery on me as your weak-minded Utopian deviants, this mysterious Hans Ashtar and his philosophies. You're the biggest hypocrite of them all. These evil inventions and technologies, many are yours, are they not? This world is of your creation, now you offer us all a New Beginning, of what? Obeying you'?

Dr VonHelmann still tries to convince him, 'It is a world I try to change for the better'.

'CHANGE? You mean revert'!

Dr VonHelmann had indeed created many advanced technologies when Head of Science, many of which this mysterious philosopher Hans Ashtar had warned against - the immorality of such would have dire consequence on for Earth, Utopia lost by the 21st century. But Dr VonHelmann saw his most astounding and advanced invention of all, a time-travel device called the Quantum Accelerator rod, as a way to revert all the damage done after the 20th-century. He saw the present as lost and, in a sense, sought to use technology to defeat itself: to rid the world of technology related to long-distance space travel that poisoned Earth and killed so many.

Seeing Master Jiang not relenting, Captain Kun-lee musters up all his courage to challenge him, removing a laser dagger from his side, 'I stand on the side of peace and an end to the chaos in Antarctica. I call on you, Master Jiang, to uphold honour and permit this vote for the start of negotiations. If you deny this request to invoke the Code of Honour, I challenge you to a fight to the death, dagger against dagger'!

Colonel Mason laughs, 'You? You cannot defeat the great Master Jiang. The best fighter in the world'!

Master Jiang smiles wryly, calling Kun-lee's bluff, 'Captain, you so weak-minded and easily swayed, I taught you better than this, so be it. I accept your challenge'!

Even though Captain Kun-lee is a top Enforcer, shown by his qualification for the prestigious Universal Games, he's very much outmatched. Despite his advanced years, this once Elite guard remains the best of the best. Every Enforcer owes their skills to him, including Kun-lee. This fight would pit student against teacher.

Pretoria tries to intervene again, 'Space Soldier coming and you make bad decision, stay with Council. Machines take over world - will make many dead'.

Master Jiang dismisses him again, 'Quiet, simpleton'.

Pretoria shakes his head, mere words have no effect on him. He's as tough as they come, a once feral orphan boy of Queen Elizabeth's slums, Pretoria was never taught to write and read. His incredible strength and determination kept him alive until he was adopted by the NEA. They would become his family as he rose up to become their leader in the capital. Unlike many others, he is not a Utopian. Still, he shares Dr VonHelmann's vision of a better world and knows the importance of loyalty and strong alliances.

Colonel Mathieu takes the brave decision to back Captain Kun-lee, drawing to a close the debate, 'All has been said. Let it be so... A fight to the death, dagger against dagger. This to decide the Enforcers' fate'.

With all weapons now lowered, they proceed to the elevator, in turn, transporting into the courtyard below. The news of this 'fight to the death' is spreading fast, and hundreds of Enforcers have already gathered. Kun-lee looks slightly bewildered, his old hesitant nature resurfacing, somewhat ruing his spur of the moment decision to pit himself against such a skilled fighter and his former professor.

Dr VonHelmann takes Captain Kun-lee to one side, doing his best to encourage for he knows a victory, however implausible, is of the utmost importance, 'We trust in you, today you show all thy strength and leadership. I see why VanWest chose you, a man of honour'.

Captain Kun-lee nods, replying, 'I do this for honour. If I die, I die with it'.

Knowing Master Jiang better than most, Dr VonHelmann offers some useful advice, 'Watch out for his counter, do not leave thyself exposed, and do NOT hesitate when given a chance, kill, WIN'.

Captain Dell, still sore from Pretoria's knocks, offers to moderate as pulsating green bars shoot up from the floor to transform the hexagon-shaped section of the courtyard into a cage.

Upon entering, only the victor will leave, Kun-lee's performance determining the future of his fellow Enforcers as well as his own.

Master Jiang has only been an academy professor for close to a century, having earned his role by protecting Dr King. During his time as an Elite guard, he prevented many assassinations attempts. Indeed, Dr King is the leader of the Council in part thanks to him. However, unbeknownst to all, Dr VonHelmann's words have affected him, he hides his human feelings well; burdened with the weight of being part of many questionable and heinous deeds he too objects to cyborgs replacing the Enforcers - those he taught

'Fight, fight'! The Enforcers start to chant as the two ready inside the hexagon.

The pulsating bars shine even brighter, ominously surrounding them as they step inside and square up to one another - their clothes transforming into black kung fu robes. The watching Enforcers are on edge, despite their chants, for many their feelings are mixed, on one side is their great academy professor, on the other one of their own, their Captain. They too by now know the stakes and what this fight is for.

To many surreal, this is no training simulation as the two contestants give each other a courtesy, a traditional kung fu salute. The left hand open and upwards, pressed against the right fist, followed by a slight bow to one another. As Master Jiang is given a laser dagger, a signal that the fight is about to commence, the Enforcers fall silent - a realisation that this is really happening!

Moderating, Captain Dell reads out the rules - coincidentally those created by Master Jiang himself. Raising his arm, he goes through the rules:

> *ONE - Death is only permitted by dagger.*
> *TWO - If the dagger is lost, both must return to their half and wait to recommence on my instruction.*
> *THREE - Only the dagger can inflict damage, there are no kicks, punches or anything else similar permitted'.*

Pausing briefly before reading the final, fatal rule,

FOUR - No-one can leave the hexagon until one is killed.

Captain Dell looks at each before dropping his arm, 'It's go time'!

His tactic one of all-out attack, Captain Kun-lee wastes no time and lunges at Master Jiang, who with a smile calmly sidesteps before acrobatically rolling forward and behind Kun-lee. The Master next mockingly swipes at Kun-lee to force him to jump away. Kun-lee is undeterred and lunges once more at Master Jiang but again misses. Even in this small hexagon, he's unable to get close, each lunge leaving him more vulnerable to the counter that Dr VonHelmann warned him about as Master Jiang saunters around as if assessing and marking Kun-lee's technique.

Master Jiang knows Kun-lee's all-out attack requires an extremely high level of stamina to maintain. And with extraordinary agility for a man his age, his plan to tire out Kun-lee is working, dodging every attack he simply waits for his opponent to slow. Now slightly confused and disorientated, Kun-lee mistakenly thinks he has corralled Master Jiang into one of the corners, lunging at him once again, this time with a vertical slice down towards his head he leaves himself open. Dr VonHelmann gasping at what he sees.

Agh! Master Jiang strikes and thrusts his dagger into his hip, causing Kun-lee to stumble backwards and drop his dagger. It doesn't look good!

Following rule 2, the fight is halted, with Master Jiang returning to his half as a wounded Kun-lee is instructed to pick up his dagger. Pretoria and Dr VonHelmann fear the worst. But this prompts the Enforcers to resume their chanting, backing and urging Kun-lee on, 'Fight! Fight Captain Kun-lee'!

Master Jiang is poised to win; only a decisive blow is needed to finish off a wounded and enervated Kun-lee, whose blood starts to stain his black clothes. Strangely though, as Captain Dell drops his arm to recommence, Master Jiang doesn't move. Instead, he looks across at the Enforcers, their passionate chants for Captain Kun-lee unsettling him. Once his student, he has never stood opposed to them, his mission for the last century was to guide them as their professor. Gone is his calm demeanour and confidence; he is saddened to see so many turn on him.

Walking up slowly to Kun-lee, he lifts his dagger over his head, leaving his body wide open for a counter. Kun-lee too disorientated to notice the change in Master Jiang's behaviour takes the opportunity to strike, thrusting his dagger forward and piercing his professor's chest.

Master Jiang staggers back, it looks like he has decided to end his life. Turning to the Enforcers, he delivers a final poignant message, 'My time has past... This present is yours. Enforcers, make from it your future'! He slumps to the floor - dead. Dr VonHelmann and Pretoria stare at each other in disbelief and elation.

Captain Kun-lee is too injured and exhausted to understand his victory has come by 'suicide by dagger', rather than 'death by dagger'. It is nevertheless a monumental victory that will send shockwaves across the solar system, a hard blow against the Universal Council. With the Commissioner in New Jersey and Dr King on Mars, there is no one left to stop the Enforcers casting their vote for talks with the NEA; in what could prove to be a watershed moment in the struggle for control of Antarctica and the success of the 'New Beginning'.

In the end, Master Jiang was unable to reconcile his loyalty for Dr King with that of seeing his Enforcers turning against him - knowing they too would be disposed of. The Council was his life, his whole reason to exist for close to 600 years. Humans were never meant to live forever, his own life covering that of 12 generations of citizens. Immortality being one of the reasons that the Universal Council's reign has lasted so very long - the Elites never dying.

The pulsating green bars disappear as Captain Dell races in to catch an injured Captain Kun-lee who stumbles forward onto the floor, Pretoria and Dr VonHelmann following in next. With no medical bots around, Dell removes an aluminium bandage from a medical kit to staunch the bleeding. Kun-lee has lost a lot of blood but is fortunate that Master Jiang's dagger missed his vital organs. The Enforcers' chants cease, they now look dumbfounded and unsure what will come next. Only a short while ago did they lose their hero Colonel Cornelius, now their academy professor Master Jiang is gone.

Pretoria crouches down and takes Kun-lee's hand, pressing it against his chest, honouring him, 'You make great man. Friend of NEA'.

Captain Kun-lee has won the Enforcers their first free vote: the Enforcers able to decide freely on a ceasefire. Against the odds, Dr VonHelmann and the EaRA, an alliance of NEA and Utopian could grow to include the Enforcers with further talks, making them more able to counter the still much more formidable Space Army. If the vote is successful and VanWest can find Dr King and cut the snake's head from its body, killing the leader of the Universal Council, then there is a chance at victory. This 'New Beginning' realised.

With Colonel Mathieu watching, Dr VonHelmann requests him to act as soon as possible before the Commissioner can intervene, 'Colonel, this is the time to act, authorise this vote. It must be NOW'!

Master Jiang's death will surely bring a massive response, including the Commissioner's contingent of Space Soldiers coming to this HQ to re-assert control. Colonel Mason is yet to respond, but if he chooses to side with the Council then Enforcer could be pitted against Enforcer as well as Space Soldier. Unprecedented!

Colonel Mathieu responds quickly - authorising a first vote for a ceasefire. A vote never thought possible now gives all Enforcers six hours to decide their 'future'. Much more is at stake than a ceasefire, their choice stark, one a fight for survival the other capitulation - their replacement by the Space Soldiers. A ceasefire would mark the end of the Universal Council's control over them.

A message scrolls across the Enforcers' Moggle Xs, *Return Your Vote For Ceasefire With NEA. 1. YES. 2. NO. 06:00:00 To REPLY.*

Chapter 5 PATH

'Why you disrespect me? Why you disrespect PATH'! Method A shouts angrily from the bar area to Commissioner Ming, who stands at the entrance of Gambler's Den.

His small contingent of Space Soldiers surveys the casino floor and their red beady eyes scan Method A's guards, having already neutralised the bouncers at the arched doorway. Oddly smiling, the Commissioner walks calmly towards Method A, along the red carpet and up the stairs, so confident that her Jerseyan guards would not dare to lay a finger on him.

Only Elites are permitted to enter New Jersey, and then only unarmed and without an escort. There has never been an infraction of the PATH agreement like this before. With the chaos engulfing Antarctica, one would think that risking a war with the Jerseyans would be the last thing the Universal Council would want to do. But these aren't normal times, and VanWest is no ordinary *Most Wanted* - his price and those he came with worth more moolah than Method A could ever dream of.

Commissioner Ming makes it clear what he wants, 'The humans where are they'?

Method A wonders how the Commissioner knows about their coming; did one of the lower Elites tip him off, or was it a Jerseyan, or something else altogether?

New Jersey is a formidable fortress. Its subway network stretches from its most westerly point, Newark Penn station, also known as 'the exit', controlled by Method A, to its most easterly point, New York, controlled by warlord Gangs Hater. Its total population reaching close to seven million. Living so deep underground, it is well protected from both the high radiation and heat as well as other threats, few weapons can penetrate its surface.

The Jerseyans are not naïve, always wary of the Universal, they know full well about their deceitfulness and bloodthirst. Over the millennia, they bore witness to the Council's takeover of the solar system. So far, their street smarts have kept them from living like that of Earth's citizens as much as their physical adaptations and their super drug, Papini.

Method A plays dumb, 'Only Jerseyans, descendants here, Commissioner'!

Warlord, come... Come now. Be sure not to take a gamble with me. You dare to risk this all, Newark and Gambler's Den, for some land people', Commissioner Ming replies plainly not believing her.

'Nah... Looksie around, no land peeps around here. Respect'? Method A keeps a poker face, not flinching despite his threat.

The Commissioner continues to smile but is not amused by her lie, 'When you have lived as many years as I, you cannot be so easily fooled. I warn, do respect the all-knowing Universal Council'!

Method A clenches her fist, she responds forcefully, 'I lose respect, you break the PATH. LEAVE Commissioner, we gonna butt heads'!

The Commissioner's smile finally vanishes, he threatens again, this time citing the third commandment, 'Be wise to know your place, Method A... In case you feel emboldened by the insurrection in Antarctica, be sure to remember all who defy the Universal Council will be destroyed'!

Method A knows she is in danger and must act, as he finishes speaking she looks over at her guards and throws up a hang loose shaka sign - the middle three digits clenched, the thumb and little finger pointing up and away. Indicating for them to get ready for a confrontation.

The Commissioner steps forward, demanding her to submit, 'Tell me, do you defy'?

Method A has her answer ready, jumping forward she headbutts the Commissioner in the chin - *clack*, knocking him down to the floor. Her guards simultaneously turn their Electrozappers on the Space Soldiers, who react in kind, entering into a deadly firefight. Clearly outmatched, the Jerseyans only hope is to slow their foe's advance, to allow their boss to retreat. They fight with desperate courage as shots whizz all around. Method A turns and hurriedly pulls down the lever of an inactive slot machine, opening up another hidden escape route.

It jolts forward to reveal a passageway. In New Jersey, there are many paths and tunnels, built so the Jerseyans can move around quickly and escape when needed, helping to protect themselves from rivals and raiding parties. Method A hopes to escape into the PATH network, to go from Newark Penn station to the next stop, Harrison, where her cousin, warlord Method Bee, is located. Only two of her guards manage to follow her inside.

An infuriated Commissioner Ming lifts himself up and immediately orders the Space Soldiers to swarm all of Newark, imposing 'Universal law'. A bloody clampdown has commenced. Powerful strikes from the SCC-300 follow, pounding the surface as Method A hurries through as bits of bricks and mortar break loose and fall over her, her drooping and wrinkled skin doing well to protect her eyes. The tunnel should be too small and narrow for the larger Space Soldiers to pass through, but their metallic limbs are able to elongate forward. Able to twist and flatten their bodies, they continue chasing.

But the PATH network is a labyrinth that the Jerseyans know best how to navigate, Method A believes it will give her a more advantageous position to repel the Space Soldiers. Better still, king scorpions like Ken and Barbie will be able to help.

A communication comes through on Method A's earpiece, it's her cousin Method Bee. The line not yet jammed by the Universal Council, her cousin is understandably shocked, 'Cousin A speak to me! The Soldiers 've gone crazy, firing down on Newark'.

A panting Method A replies, resigned to the fact she is unable to hold her territory, 'Newark lost... The crazy Universal broke the PATH. We at war'!

Method Bee offers his help, 'Get to Harrison. I got the backup, lots and lots of shooters, aye'?

She is already on her way, thanking him, 'You good, Bee. Coming'!

Method Bee relays too a message he has received, 'This Commissioner says Universal law in place. Says cease and do not engage'.

Simultaneously, they say, 'No way'! They will not submit to any intruder, however powerful.

Despite the brave efforts of her remaining two guards to slow the Space Soldiers, they continue to gain ground. Even blowing up the walls behind does little to stop them, the Soldiers' hands able to morph into rippers and blades, they shift the fallen bricks and mortar out of the way with ease. Method A uses her superior knowledge of the tunnel's layout to swing left and slide down a ventilation shaft.

Landing on her feet on the rail tracks, she receives a long and worrying message from Gs next, having only just managed to slip by the Commissioner's SCC-300 - *In Orbit Cloaked. Not Detected. Huge Ass SSC, Spaceships Firing Down On Newark. Thx Cancel My Wheel Debts. Stay Safe Boss.*

* * * * *

Too busy trying to save her own skin, Method A does not respond. Waiting for a mining cart, she scrapes from the wall some raw Papini, which she grinds up in her hands and scoffs down, giving her a much-needed boost that also calms her nerves. *Screech!* A cart finally arrives to pick her up. Hopping inside, the cart quickly accelerates in the direction of Harrison. The carts are frequent, so if any of her remaining two guards make it this far, then there should be another coming to pick them up.

The bombardment is now so intense that, despite being deep underground, it shakes here too. Slowing her progress are dozens of Jerseyans who flee for their lives in the same direction. Notwithstanding the delay, she makes good speed and soon reaches Harrison station, the next stop on the PATH network, where a heavily armed Method Bee waits. Having blockaded the tracks with several overturned carts, the warlord of Harrison is ready for an attack. And with him are over 500 heavily armed Jerseyans, plus hundreds of king scorpions hidden in the nooks and crannies of the tunnel walls. The sound of heavy footsteps rises - the Space Soldiers are close.

Method A arrives shocked and puzzled, in disbelief that her refusal to hand over this 'traitor' VanWest could have caused the Universal Council to break PATH. By establishing 'Universal law', they want to subjugate and control New Jersey, the chaos of Antarctica spreading across Earth. She also worries about VanWest's warning that even more Space Soldiers are amassing to come to Earth. And knows that she needs more allies.

Method A throws up a shaka sign as she hops out of the cart and gives her cousin a chest bump. The rest of Harrison's Jerseyans return the sign in salute. However, before they can speak, a flash of light illuminates the tunnel behind her, forcing her to duck.

Screech! She looks back as another bolt of light crashes into a wall close by, a cart is coming, this one belonging to her trusted guard, Bruva Tee. He struggles to slow it down as the heavy footsteps behind him hasten. Soon in view are dozens of Space Soldiers, they sprint in one long column at what must be more than 60 miles per hour.

'Warning, resistance is futile, respect Universal law. Cease and do not engage, must comply', the Space Soldiers repeat robotically, ordering the Jerseyans to lay down their arms and surrender.

Waiting behind the overturned carts, Harrison's fighters brace for battle and to engage as the Space Soldiers come closer. Many are armed with Subway Hunters, a specially adapted Plasma blaster made for the smaller, Jerseyan hands. Not too dissimilar to the Enforcer's Corner Shot, whose shots travel around corners and chase their targets.

Boom! Coming into range, Method Bee signals for his fighters to fire the first volley. The Space Soldiers continue undeterred, hardly flinching even when struck. Method A is quick to take shelter behind an overturned cart with Method Bee, she needs to discuss with her cousin about getting more support to fight the Universal Council. But it is difficult to talk, the flashes of light and the noise becoming ever more disorientating as the Space Soldiers fire back even more aggressively than before. Falling bricks throwing up more dust into the air.

'We gotta go see Rulez Haah. Go to Journal Square, aye'? Method A poses the question to Method Bee. Rulez Haah, the powerful warlord of the east side of New Jersey.

'Aye, but Rulez Haah bit crazy'! Method Bee replies, unsure how she will react to their request for help.

This warlord is not known to be the most hospitable, Method Bee has had several minor clashes with her before, including incursions for moolah and displays of dominance. However, these invading Space Soldiers leave them with no other recourse: they are outmatched. They are only a vanguard probing for weaknesses - more will come. To reach her they must go to Journal Square station, taking them through the dangerous no-man's-land of Turnpike. The Jerseyan's lands are roughly split as follows by four warlords, among the PATH network:

- *Newark Penn 'The Exit' - Method A*
- *Harrison - Method Bee*
- *Turnpike - no-man's-land*
- *Journal Square to Exchange Place and Hoboken - Rulez Haah*
- *Christopher Street and World Trade Center (Manhattan) - Gangs Hater*

Boom! A new series of shots strike their cart, badly damaging it and removing their protection. The Space Soldiers are only yards away now, they must engage.

'Let's mow these machines down'! Method A shouts.

Method Bee signals for all his fighters and king scorpions to charge; in unison, the Jerseyans jump over their overturned carts and fire everything they got at the Space Soldiers. The king scorpions crawl out from the walls to join the fight, catching them by surprise as they leap on top. Their powerful claws clamping onto their metal limbs, and stingers striking down from above - albeit their venom has little effect on the cyborgs.

More support arrives. Having followed from Newark Penn station, Ken emerges from behind with more scorpions - though without his partner Barbie who stays out of this fight to protect their babies. These tunnels are as much their home as the Jerseyans. The Space Soldiers are pinned in, those at the sides locked in claw-to-blade combat with the scorpions, and those in front exchanging fire with the Jerseyans.

Even with the king scorpions helping, the Jerseyans still struggle to progress against the formidable Space Soldiers - many struck down in quick succession. Ken manages to progress, adroitly dodging a volley of shots as he reaches one, pulling it down. But it takes more than 5 king scorpions to finally snap a Space Soldier's limb off. Knowing the odds are against them, the Soldiers sound the retreat, hacking their way through the king scorpions to withdraw, who continue to snap and sting.

Seeing this, Method A and Bee halt the Jerseyan advance. It doesn't feel like a victory, rather the beginning of more fighting.

Beep-beep! A most ominous sound can be heard: the neutralised Space Soldiers beeping loudly. Method A instinctively grabs Bee and pulls him down behind some fallen rubble. *Kaboom!* The neutralised Space Soldiers explode, taking out whole swathes of king scorpions, who hiss loudly in pain, as well as many Jerseyans. The flames sweeping through the tunnel, Ken is just able to take shelter as he crawls into a crack.

Method A's quick reaction has saved not only her own life but also her cousin's, they re-emerge as the flames pass to find a scene of utter destruction. Close to 100 fighters and king scorpions have perished. The Space Soldiers having left a cunning and sick trap: forcing so many to amass for maximum damage. Her last loyal guard, Bruva Tee, is one of those mortally wounded, he lays on the floor gasping his last breaths. Her ears still ringing, Method A staggers over to comfort him.

Placing her hand on his wrinkled forehead, 'Bruva Tee, thank you, the little ones I take care of always, aye'. Drawing his final breath and closing his eyes, she eulogises, 'Go feast now in the Chamber of Warriors'. A Jerseyan belief that warriors transcend to a great feasting hall upon their deaths.

Staggering back over to the overturned carts, Method Bee and Method A put up a shaka sign in respect and homage, the remaining fighters and king scorpions gathering around. Fortunately, most of the king scorpions have survived protected by their hard chitin exoskeleton and quick retreat into the cracks. Their bravery and sacrifice has saved many Harrison Jerseyans as well as those seeking refuge from Newark. With the bombardment overhead only intensifying, they know another attack is coming. And, as expected, the last few refugees confirm that Commissioner Ming has taken full control of Newark, disabling all communication lines.

Method A and Bee instruct the fighters to hold the station as they go for help, 'Stay strong, we gonna go to Journal Square. Aye'!

'Aye'! Many badly wounded, their resolve remains strong.

The Method cousins climb inside a metal mining cart further down the tracks, which promptly rolls eastwards in the direction of Journal Square station. Ken follows with a few other king scorpions to provide protection through Turnpike's no-man's-land. They hope to find a hospitable Rulez Haah, she is more powerful than them and maintains a much larger territory. News of the PATH infraction will have surely reached her by now.

'Jerseyans' is a collective term used by outsiders, internally they refer to each other by their PATH station - seeing each other very much as rivals rather than one homogeneous group. Separating the warlords is Turnpike, it is filled with tens of thousands of homeless Jerseyans. Many are vagrants, gambling addicts and those addicted to the highly concentrated, hallucinogenic form of Papini called Liquid Blue: a scourge that starts to inflict many in the Antarctic settlements as well. Living in Newark and Harrison is tough, living in Turnpike is fatal: sooner or later your number is bound to be up.

As they speed on, the only positive of the bombardment above is its effect on the vagrants, who cower away and do not attack, allowing them to pass through the tracks unimpeded. The distance is far longer than that of Newark Penn to Harrison, they watch as thousands upon thousands of eyes stare back at them, lost and unknowing of what comes next - 'Universal law' spreading eastwards from Newark.

Finally entering Rulez Haah's territory, Method A signals to Ken and the other king scorpions to wait at the border. Their metal cart slowing as they approach Journal Square. Here the walls do not vibrate, and there is no bombardment, the Commissioner yet to attack. Lining the platform are dozens of heavily armed fighters, visibly on edge at seeing two rival warlords arrive after the news of all that has transpired. They point their arms at them as their cart comes to a halt. Several king scorpions emerge from the walls, hissing and rubbing their two front claws over their heads, their stingers pointing menacingly down at them.

The cousins immediately hold their hands up to signal that they come in peace. Method A calls out, 'Come to speak with Rulez Haah, aye'!

They wait several long, tense minutes as neither moves. The cousins are unsure of what is going to happen to them next. But then a strange rhythmic sound breaks the silence - *Bam-tap-bing!* The sound of hollow metal pipes being knocked against each other, signalling Rulez Haah's arrival. Coming down the platform are four strapping young Jerseyans, their near-transparent skin showing as they carry a palanquin, encircled in bright red curtains. She sits inside on top equally bright red cushions, her hair bright-purple and her face partially hidden behind a burgundy laced veil.

With her guard's weapons still locked on them, they are ushered out of the cart and onto the platform to follow the palanquin. Escorting them up a flight of grey, concrete stairs, they enter into a lavish well-decorated floor of the station. The walls are bedecked with ornate portraits, many of which seem to belong to the same family, each with a characteristic frill neck and double chin, many too sport purple hair.

Walking through beaded curtains, they are greeted by scantily dressed servants. The Method cousins are somewhat relieved, it looks like a hospitable reception. With the palanquin placed down on a blue-tiled floor, more servants rush in carrying delicious looking bowls of multi-coloured Papini, which they lay in its centre. There isn't just one type, the usual white powder form, but several: red, yellow, pink and violet. Each with its own nutritional value and packed with much-needed vitamins, minerals and antioxidants that help to decrease and reverse the effects of radiation poisoning. Also served is enoki wine, also known as flammulina velutipes wine, an alcoholic drink made from mushrooms.

Bam-tap-bing! The same coarse beat plays again as Rulez Haah finally steps out. The carriers are taking handfuls of the Papini powder and shower it over her as she makes her way to a round and pink silk cushion. She is ostentatiously dressed, her flabby skin pierced with rings of diamonds and decorated with tattoos of king scorpions.

She addresses them, offering each a cushion, 'Methods... I expected you to come'. She seeks to take advantage not realising the gravity of the situation, 'We not always see eye-to-eye, but I'm forgiving Rulez. You come for my help, to make deal, aye'?

Method A replies first, trying to lead the conversation to one of collaboration, 'Dawg, we need to team-up. They too strong, defeat us station by station if not'!

But Rulez Haah disagrees strongly, 'Nah! They've come for you, looksie around... They not here! This problem yours, aye'!

Method Bee stops Method A answering further, trying to keep the conversation cordial, 'Great warlord Rulez Haah, believe us. You see our peeps fleeing, aye'?

Rulez Haah shakes her head, still believing the issue to be theirs alone as she makes her audacious offer, 'Nah! This fight is about you helping that traitor, VanWest. You need my help. I offer good deal... Give me Harrison, Newark... I speak to Universal Council. Tell them big misunderstanding. You give them VanWest, serve me. Simple, aye'?

Method A shakes her head, 'You silly dawg... This VanWest is long gone. Commissioner, Space Army come to Journal. There is nothing to bargain for, no deal to make. There is only one choice: team up or die'!

Still, Rulez Haah does not understand, removing her veil, she looks lustfully at Method Bee and amends her deal slightly, 'Hmm, new deal, I take that wrinkled Bee, make him mine... Harrison, Bee mine, you give Universal VanWest. Best offer'.

But as she finishes speaking, the ground starts to vibrate, and a heavily armed Jerseyan comes bursting in, his name Bruva Lem, he pants heavily, 'Me sorry, my boss... many Space Soldiers on the roof of Transportation Center... say Universal law in place'!

'What'? A shocked Rulez Haah jumps up.

'Message that "you MUST comply", report to Commissioner and handover the Method cousins. Say Gangs Hater make the right decision. Wise to follow'.

It appears that Manhattan's warlord Gangs Hater has already capitulated and sided with the Universal Council. A seething Rulez Haah turns to Method A, blaming her again, 'This all because of you'!

This infraction of PATH marks an even more serious escalation. Rulez Haah controls the largest and most powerful territory, with it much of the Papini trade and over a thousand cargo ships that regularly trade with the Elites. Daring to challenge her means PATH is officially over and the anonymous status of the Jerseyans gone.

Chapter 6 The Red Planet

VanWest rouses from his sleep covered in sweat and the awful mustardy stench from the Papini bags. Greeting him is a smiling, pointy-toothed Gs and his sweet Iris.

'It zero five Arcadia time! Look out the window at Mars', Gs welcomes VanWest in his squeaky voice, it's dawn in the trading post of Arcadia Plains, they have arrived!

'You are such a sound sleeper'! Iris jokes as she leans into his crate to give him a gentle kiss on the forehead.

They have made it to the red planet, and it seems that Gs has kept true to his word and not betrayed them. VanWest lifts himself up and steps out the crate, keen to look through the viewing glass and see the planet of his origins for the first-time. Rubbing his bleary eyes, the effect of Gs's blue sleeping pill still to fully wear off, before walking over to have a look.

Arcadia Plains is situated in the MC-03 zone, in the volcanic plains. An area covered by a sea of lava, its colours even more vivid than those around the Island of Crete, the location of the Universal Games. The sight is spectacular, spews of bright red and yellow lava clash to send dense plumes of ash over 60 miles into the air. VanWest wonders how anyone can live in such a chaotic landscape but they do. The volcanos were said to be dormant for millions of years and then somehow became active again in recent times. The Universal Council's Wiki simply calling it a natural phenomenon.

Looking across, VanWest spots the trading post perched on an elevated rock between the lava streams. All the inhabitants are sheltered inside an enormous crystalline dome that provides them with breathable air and protection from the harmful and radioactive particles found in Mars's low gravity atmosphere. The dome, like the one on the Moon's Clavius Crater trading post, is not magnetic but constructed from a silica aerogel compound. A material that lets through 97% of light, whilst blocking harmful UV light and radioactive particles, a lower-tech and cheaper alternative to magnetism.

Gs cargo ship is headed to its port, where they will disembark. From there, they must find a navigable route to the hidden base in Alba Mons, all whilst remaining undetected. Even with Earth's insurrection, this trading post should not be too heavily guarded, for few live and work here. Its only use as a provisioning point for prisoner transport vessels and Jerseyan cargo ships before travelling onwards to the mining colonies.

Fortunate to escape New Jersey as Universal law came into place they are also lucky that Gs's cargo ship has not been stopped or destroyed on the way. In part thanks to the technicality of his ship not being registered as the property of either Method cousin. SOS messages are coming in from hundreds of ships licensed to them that they have been placed in lockdown and impounded, some even destroyed.

LeSouris comes over to greet VanWest, keen to commence planning their next steps. With the rush to escape Newark and Gambler's Den, all he knows is that VanWest has coordinates for this base, with little detail on how to reach it or what they will do if and when they find Dr King. Handing him a box of nutritional pills and a flask of Gs' mushroom water, a drink packed with protein and other minerals, LeSouris checks that they are out of Gs's earshot before speaking. This time it is him that is most anxious.

Whispering, 'My friend... We make it to red planet undetected. We must praise. But plan, what is it'?

Not enjoying the mushroom water's tangy taste, VanWest whispers back, 'I cannot quite say, not yet'.

VanWest senses something that he cannot put into words, a voice calling, compelling him on. Inside this base, there is something he knows will help him. Iris comes over to join the conversation, putting her arm around his waist, she has good news to share, 'Pretoria and my father met with Captain Kun-lee. There's a vote for a ceasefire. He hopes for them to become Free Enforcers. And with a little more persuasion to join in the New Beginning'.

'This is wonderful'! VanWest exclaims.

'It is. Praise be'! LeSouris adds.

There is more, 'Big news too... This Master Jiang is dead'.

VanWest jaw drops momentarily, taking a few seconds to recompose himself, he answers, 'Master Jiang! Are you sure'?

'A fight to the death with a Captain... Kun-lee'.

VanWest's reaction catches the attention of Gs, who curiously looks over at them. The moment is bittersweet, his one-time professor who he owes much of his skills to is dead, but it has won the Enforcers a free vote. If successful, Earth's Resistance Army (EaRA) will be better placed to withstand the mighty Space Army, to counter a fleet up to nine hundred spaceships strong. If they were to join this 'New Beginning' and the EaRA and he could kill Dr King, victory might even be a possibility.

LeSouris has more, not wholly unexpected, news, 'Pretoria writes this Colonel Mason objects, Enforcer could be fighting Enforcer. I hear too that Commissioner becomes even crazier, Space Soldiers attack not just Gambler's Den, attack all of East Side'!

VanWest looks back through the viewing portal, he feels the burden of fulfilling their part in the success of this 'New Beginning'. He replies, 'Dr VonHelmann has done so well... A vote, it's incredible. It is our turn to deliver'.

A curious Gs steps beside and asks them, 'This base'? The trio freeze, being so careless to allow themselves to be overheard, they are unsure how to reply.

'Universal broke PATH, they come with Soldiers and guns, your enemy, my enemy. The Method cousins, A, Bee, fight Commissioner and Soldiers'.

Iris sees the opportunity to work together and the opportunity to expand the EaRA further with the Jerseyans as allies, 'I hope they succeed. Tell them to contact Pretoria, the NEA can help'!

Gs smiles, 'Aye! It's hard to message, comms blocked... I gonna try'.

Iris takes the risky decision to reveal details of their daring mission, 'Gs, we appreciate all you have done. We need to go to Alba Mons. Can you help us'?

VanWest points at his holomap and gives even more detail, 'We believe that Dr King has fled to this place, there's a hidden base underneath this mountain'.

'Really? Dr King! Nah! My map shows no base there. It's quiet'!

LeSouris presses further, 'My friend, VanWest's source is reliable. Trust'.

Gs explains the plan, 'Hmm, ok Sour. Listen up, medicine sista, health inspector alter your DNA to get you through port... she got trick to transport you out of dome next'.

'That sounds promising'! Iris responds, looking at LeSouris and VanWest for their opinion. But VanWest is wary.

Gs makes clear that it comes at an additional cost, 'Sista needs your moolah first. Dome is difficult... She works for no boss. Hear you lots of moolah, show me moolah, make it happen'.

LeSouris wants to first clarify his concerns about the DNA altering, 'My friend, Gs. This DNA altering, I have heard of before when smuggling but I never use, it harms us'?

'Nah! It's safe. Sista Cee is the bomb'. He continues, 'DNA thang is part of package to Mars... Nifty trick out dome cost extra'.

Iris struggles to understand Gs thick Jerseyan dialect, she asks, 'What is this trick exactly'?

'Keep secret safe... Sista has old school Magicbox. Transports little thangs in, out of dome. Good deal, aye'?

Iris responds, with a hint of concern in her voice, 'I know it'.

The Magicbox is the precursor to the transportation hub. It is said to be quite dangerous and unpredictable, but over short distances, it usually works. It's not ideal, but getting out of Arcadia Plains is imperative to the mission, and this seems to be their best option.

VanWest looks nervously at LeSouris, wondering if he actually has any 'moolah' to barter with. LeSouris has already spent a hefty sum, a large pink diamond, to get them thus far; he has nothing left of value.

LeSouris checks to see if Gs is bluffing, asking him, 'My friend, we have no more moolah. Method A would not send us here only for us to get captured, yes? Want me to contact and ask what my lovely pink diamond paid for'?

Gs shakes his head and returns a derisory look, he has spotted something of value and points at Iris's ring. Whatever agreement made between him and his boss ends at the port. Knowing them to be *Most Wanted*, he has already risked a lot to get them even to this point. And this payment isn't for him, it is for this 'sista'.

'Risk a lot to get you here. This new deal for Sista Cee... that blue-green rock looks top. She has, aye'?

LeSouris turns to a surprised Iris, 'What you think'?

Albeit emeralds are not that valuable, this one's rare colour makes it quite exceptional. Iris is understandably reluctant to see it go, to her this gift from her father is priceless, one of only two pieces of jewellery ever given to her by him.

But with the success of their mission at stake, she agrees, 'My father gave it to me, he will understand. I think... I hope'.

'Da ring top, Sista Cee will be happy', Gs answers with a smile.

Having lost the amber stone pendant to the Interrogator, VanWest feels especially bad for Iris, 'My sweet, you cannot... we can find something else'. But Iris has already made her decision, removing her ring she hands it to Gs.

LeSouris clarifies the terms of their new deal, 'Sista Cee give us DNA alteration to escape port and Magicbox to escape the dome. Correct, yes'?

'Aye, Sour. This correct'! Gs nods.

With their negotiation concluded, the cargo ship starts its powered descent into the landing zone, its domed roof opens on their approach. A message rolls across the holomap, *Universal Jurisdiction. Cargo Arrivals Bay. Await Check. Must Comply.*

Gs is a little taken aback and looks at LeSouris, he had not expected this port to be on high alert.

With the ship landing, Gs briefly explains again what will happen next, 'I get Sista Cee. After health check, you exit, go to her office, Magicbox'.

LeSouris nods, giving VanWest and Iris a reassuring smile, 'Trust in Utopia'!

Given the Jerseyan love of moolah, VanWest still worries that Gs will be tempted to betray them. Their fates, that of the citizens, the success of the 'New Beginning', now rests in the hands of a gambler and smuggler. None has any weapon to defend themselves, having barely escaped Gambler's Den before the Commissioner and the Space Soldiers stormed Newark. VanWest takes a little comfort that he hasn't foreseen a problem, but then again, he knows that his visions remain quite random and, for the most part, not under his control. As LeSouris said, they must now 'trust'.

Gs closes his visor and exits the ship, telling them as he leaves, 'Keep low, touch nothing, enjoy some Papini'!

Good advice, they will need it to acclimatise. LeSouris grabs a bag of Papini powder from his crate and empties it onto its lid. Whilst the dome keeps the air breathable, it nevertheless remains quite toxic. Unbeknownst to VanWest, he has had this powder many times before, albeit in capsule form. Not only used in the prisoner colonies, but the Universal Council have also added it as a secret, vital supplement to the strict Enforcer diet. One that helped him to maintain optimal performance during his tours of the settlements.

On Mars, Papini is more of a necessity than an enhancer. Space Soldiers will not be their only issue, its carbon dioxide atmosphere is hostile to humanoid species. Outside of the dome, they would die of hypoxia within minutes without it. Another threat they have yet to plan for is the freezing conditions, being much further from the sun than Earth, the temperature will drop dramatically as they leave the volcanic plains. Alba Mons is not an active volcano, rather an ice-cold mountain.

After licking up a line, VanWest's mind becomes stimulated and focused, he checks his Quantum Communicator, but there are no messages. His vision on the journey to Mars is still very much on his mind. He wonders if it has a special importance to his mission, his coming here. Remembering what Dr VonHelmann had shown him of Mars's first settlement, he quietly checks the holomap for the location of the file tagged *Mars One, Cydonia.* Certain that is where this church is located, at least its ruin: this the site where the Martian President Van der Westhuizen and his daughter died.

He tries multiple search terms, including *First Settlement, Cydonia*, but nothing returns. Recalling interesting Mars facts from the Universal Council's Wiki, he checks for the 'Face of Mars' mountain, famed for its uncanny resemblance to a human face. Maybe this is a sign of civilisation and zooms in on its coordinates: *Northern Hemisphere, Arabia MC-12 zone, geolocation 8-77.* However, he finds no trace of human activity. All that exists are miles and miles of rocks and red sand.

Creak! The opening of the ship's lift doors interrupts, causing them all to scramble behind the Papini crates. They wait to see who will come - hoping for the best.

Chapter 7 Arcadia Plains and the Magicbox

Gs returns, accompanied by an even shorter Jerseyan. This must be Sista Cee, who happily wears Iris's emerald ring as a bracelet, her hands and fingers being tinier than a human's. Being the Jerseyan health inspector, her official role is to screen new arrivals. To the trio's relief, the lift doors close behind with no one else following. It looks like Gs hasn't sold them out and the Universal Council hasn't singled out his ship for any aggressive inspection, at least not yet. With her help, they must alter their DNA, disguising themselves to pass through the port.

Sista Cee's Jerseyan features are more pronounced than Gs, her face and neck covered in layers of see-through skin that resemble fish gills. A mutation come evolutionary upgrade that helps Jerseyans to filter and purify the radioactive air. This adaptation also perfectly suits them for long-distance space travel to other planets, including Mars. A planet not too dissimilar to Earth and New Jersey in the year 3000.

Tucked under Sista Cee's arm is a small chrome box labelled *Gamma Blood Test Kit*, wherein are hidden the tools for their alteration.

LeSouris is the first to emerge from behind the crates, 'Welcome'!

Gs's usual smiley face is gone, he warns, 'We gotta hustle! Security high, Inspector comes soon. Sista Cee gonna turn you into Jerseyans fast'!

The trio hadn't quite understood this detail and look a little stunned as Sista Cee places the chrome box down and unpacks the items, including a long electro round-tipped needle and two vials of what appears to be a nearly colourless, slightly bluish blood. Jerseyan blood!

She speaks in a similar Jerseyan dialect to Gs, luckily her accent isn't so thick, 'This makes you tall Jerseyans'. And informs them, 'This last 45 minutes. Not long'!

Seeing the items being laid out, LeSouris gets some last-minute jitters, he says to Iris, 'My friend, I think I will watch first... I see what happens'.

Iris rolls her eyes, replying, 'No need to act like a farm cockroach about it'!

Causing Gs and VanWest to laugh at an embarrassed LeSouris, whose cheeks turn a little red. He's an experienced smuggler, but that also means he knows the risk of alterations. Being quite a short human, LeSouris will at least look more the part than the others. Iris offers her forearm first, which Sista Cee grabs hold of and quickly rubs her long-tipped needle against her skin. Taking only a split second to administer, there is no instant change in appearance, but Iris does feel a little queasy and has to sit-down on the floor.

VanWest goes next, the needle an unwelcome reminder of his medical checks as an Enforcer. Looking at Sista Cee and Iris, he reasons that this will feel no different to his change in appearance in 1998, Florida via the facial remodulation kit. He offers his forearm next, the Jerseyan blood is absorbed through the skin's pores. But, as he gives a reassuring smile to Iris, he notices that she is beginning to transform, her skin's pigment turning grey and her neck becoming flabbier. He looks down at his forearm and sees his skin is changing too. Throwing up orange liquid, he realises this method to be more involved than thought; it's not simply masking his DNA, it is temporarily changing it.

Agh! LeSouris lets out a small cry, aghast by their changing appearance. Iris is no longer recognisable, her skin is not even grey anymore, it has turned colourless. She looks like a bonafide Jerseyan. LeSouris looking now even less keen to follow! This veteran hacker and smuggler, who has seen many a shocking sight in his time, cannot bear to give his forearm to an impatient Sista Cee.

'Come on, bruva! Inspection coming'! Gs hurries LeSouris to offer his arm. With the trading post on high alert, he is expecting a Universal Inspector to arrive anytime now.

A dizzied VanWest also urges him on, his voice going squeaky, 'Don't be a farm cockroach! We need to move, Dr VonHelmann, Pretoria, all of Earth's citizens are counting on us'.

After a long sigh, LeSouris relents and stretches out his forearm, squeezing his eyes shut he mouths, *Trust in Utopia*!

He grimaces as he feels the needle rub against his skin, soon feeling its effect. Puking orange liquid as his body transforms, his pointy ears shrink and his skin becomes flabby and wrinkled, even more so than that of Iris and indeed that of Sista Cee! His face looking more and more like an oversized and colourless prune, shrivelled and round.

'You look good'! Gs tells him with an amused look, 'The more wrinkled, the better in Jerseyan society'.

'I know, very sexy... but this last time ever, thank you', a still coughing LeSouris replies sarcastically - his voice turning squeaky.

'Listen carefully... If this Inspector ask questions, talk like me, aye'? Drawing a small smirk from VanWest, which prompts an unamused Iris to thump him in the shoulder, unimpressed by his rudeness.

'Aye'! Iris answers, a little startled to hear her own squeaky voice.

'Aye'! VanWest follows, as does LeSouris. 'This for the New Beginning'.

Sista Cee informs them that the inspection will happen at any moment, 'They're close'!

Handing them some greyish, rag-like clothes. Gs moves to the final item, the creation of their pseudo-identities, pointing to VanWest, Iris and LeSouris, in turn, 'They ask, your names

Bruva V, Sista Eye, you, hmm... Flabby Ls. Remember, walk small like me'.

As the lift doors open, Gs directs VanWest and Iris to hunch over and pick up a crate of Papini, with LeSouris walking behind. They then follow him out of the cargo hold to await inspection. For VanWest, stepping out gives him an instant rush, a surreal feeling not too dissimilar to déjà vu; a feeling of returning home after a long absence. Regaining his composure, he surveys the port - as a well-trained Enforcer should. Gs instructs them again to keep holding the crate.

Over 20-foot tall, a bronze statue stands imposingly at the other end of the landing zone. That of a muscular man smashing a mighty hammer into an anvil, it is Vulcan the Roman God of metalwork and fire. A small inscription on its hammer, written in Latin, reads *Ad Quod Opus Hominis Progressum Ad Totam Concilium*. It is the Universal's second commandment and that of the Enforcer's motto: to work for the progression of man and the Universal. A troubling reminder of who is in charge here.

Similar to the Roman statue of Jupiter seen in Stage 1 of the Universal Games, these neoclassical statues serve an important purpose, as a display of power and to mark Universal Council territory and jurisdiction. This, in particular, a place of work. The trading post's location is smart, the lava that flows close by provides a much-needed source of energy for its operations. Mars being much further from the sun than Earth, 243 million miles to be exact, is close to minus 60 degrees celsius on average.

An inspection unit emerges from behind the statue, led by a tall, slender man dressed in a skin-tight black jumpsuit, his snake-like posture is creepily akin to that of the Interrogator. Accompanying the Universal Inspector are four patrol androids, whilst VanWest does not foresee any issue he still feels worried. The Universal Council should not be looking for them here, given this trading post's relatively minor and unknown status. Being unarmed and without support, they stand little chance of escape if discovered.

A concerned Gs whispers to them, 'If they come, bow low. Remember names, Bruva V, Sista Eye, Flabby Ls. No looksie in the eyes'.

The Inspector strides towards them, his eyes narrowing as he gets closer, looking for any minute detail out of place whilst pressing his phaser against his chest. Patrol androids zoom ahead, surrounding the ship and blocking any prospect of retreat. *Hum*! The androids commence scanning, primarily looking for concealed goods and biohazards. Their persons carefully scanned not only once, not twice, but thrice. Such is the heightened level of alert.

As Gs instructed, they say nothing, hoping that Sista Cee's DNA alteration will do the 'trick'. The Inspector keeps staring at them until each scan is complete as they bow their heads. However, for VanWest and Iris, the weight of the crate starts to wear, lactic acid building up in their arms. With the final scan complete, the Inspector places his phaser back to his side. Nothing out of the ordinary has been detected, and the Inspector's attention turns to that of a much larger ship that docks further down the landing zone.

It's a prisoner transporter, its occupants the likely recipients of Gs's Papini shipment; liquefied and injected by their handlers to prolong their lives for the grime and laborious days ahead in the mines. Even though the inspection unit begins to move away, the long wait proves too much for Iris, and she can no longer keep hold of her end of the crate. She tries to call LeSouris to come and help, but it is too late.

Bang! It comes crashing down, the lid breaking open and the bags of Papini spilling onto the ground. The Inspector turns sharply. Scowling, he removes his phaser and aims it at her wrinkled forehead. VanWest and LeSouris brace themselves, clenching their fists, ready to react if need be.

'Ss-state, state your name'? The Inspector orders, his speech very similar to that of the Interrogator who tortured VanWest on the SCC-400, also like that of a hissing snake.

A quivering Iris replies submissively, mimicking Gs's voice, 'Bruv-va, I... Sista Eye'.

Even though he is not entirely convinced, a well-timed communication causes the Inspector to disengage. Before leaving, he points down to the Papini bags, 'Be wis-se to clean, clean it'!

LeSouris and VanWest lift the crate back up, as Iris hurriedly places the bags back inside. With the Inspector out of earshot, Gs whispers to them to get going, 'Follow my Sista Cee out. Carefully carry crate, aye'.

Iris nods, and they hurry, keeping their heads bowed, to catch up with Sista Cee, who waits for them at the entrance of the transportation hub. Before it initialises, VanWest notices out of the corner of his eye that the Inspector has turned back from the prisoner transportation ship, this time striding back with his phaser pointing at Gs's forehead.

Before he can inform the others, Sista Cee instructs the tube to take them to the 'Red-light district', close to where her office is located. In a flash, they all transport. They are immediately struck by how quiet the place is, worryingly quieter than one would expect. A district popular with Jerseyan traders, who stopover to entertain themselves in one of the many Hypersphere simulators - it should be livelier than this.

VanWest has visited a similar place before, after his graduation to Enforcer. This trading post is designed similar to Clavius Crater, located on the moon. This district only permitted for Jerseyan traders, lower Elites 'the descendants', and on the moon only Enforcers on leave, on account of 'health' reasons. The simulators are said to alleviate and reverse the effects of long-distance space travel. But all of the Hypersphere pods are closed - the whole place is in lockdown.

Activating his Moggle X lenses, he spots two Quadrotors hovering in the distance, their warning lights orange, indicating that they are on the hunt. An anxious-looking Sista Cee leads them down a path to her office, which is located at the other end of the district and close to the dome's wall. Iris helps LeSouris to carry his end of the crate as they hurry on.

Daring not to speak in case they rouse the attention of the Quadrotors, they pass between two rows of lead-painted shacks. VanWest notices that his hands are shaking, a sign he has come to know as imminent danger. He looks back and realises they have been spotted, the two Quadrotors stalking them. Sweat drips down Sista Cee's wrinkled face as she ushers them into a much narrower alleyway. A clever move that buys them a few precious seconds, with the Quadrotors forced to split and fold to follow.

Sista Cee points at her office, approximately 100 meters from the dome's wall, hoping that the Magicbox will be able to transport them this distance, if not more. Adding to their haste is their skin-transforming back, less than 10 of the 45 minutes of their disguise remaining. The landing zone's inspection proving to be too time-consuming. With VanWest's bionics deactivated and masked, he hadn't set a timer on his Moggle X as per usual in one of his operations.

'Guys, I have a bad feeling', VanWest warns in a low voice.

'One of those feelings'? Iris whispers back.

Before VanWest can answer, a sweaty Sista Cee unlocks the door to her office and rushes them inside, shutting and then bolting the door behind. Wheezing and huffing, she tells them, 'I get the Magicbox', as the trio drop the crate on the floor.

Waaahhhh! A high screeching noise, a siren blares cacophonously, dropping them to their knees - a raid is imminent. The building begins to shake next as they struggle to get back to their feet. They MUST teleport. An authoritative voice looms outside, instructing that 'Universal law is in place, stay indoors or you will be arrested'.

Sista Cee opens a cupboard filled with an assortment of strange looking devices. One being the old prototype transporter, the Magicbox. Commonly used until the 27th century, whilst it worked well at teleporting inanimate objects a short distance, it was too often not so good at teleporting living objects such as humans; the device working by aiming a red laser beam and then slowly sending particles through the air at a speed of several thousand every nanosecond. Unfortunately, a number of reported cases of body parts going missing earned it a bad reputation, monikers such as the 'Magic Vanishing Box' and a 'Box Half Full'.

Sista Cee has quite the collection of devices, including a Jerseyan favourite, the Electrozapper. A primitive but effective weapon that is especially good at disabling androids and other machines. Not so much though with Space Soldiers. On the top shelf, there are rows of cans labelled 'Papini XYZ'.

With the loud commanding voice repeating for all to comply and stay indoors, Sista Cee hands LeSouris a can, 'Hyper Papini helps to breathe outside dome', instructing him to take some himself and distribute the rest as she prepares the Magicbox.

LeSouris rips open the can, its powder much whiter, purer than that of regular Papini. Pouring it on each of their hands, he instructs to lick it up like before. The sensation is intense, temporarily sending everything into slow motion - with the noise of the sirens outside disappearing and replaced with a sweet humming noise. It takes them a moment to regain their bearings.

By the time they do, Sista Cee has setup the Magicbox, with a red marker beaming out from its top. She carries the machine to the hallway and points it in the direction of the dome's outer wall, on the other side of the metal shack. VanWest has read how this prototype works in the Universal Council's Wiki, they will have to run along the beam's laser one at a time and hope it transports them before they hit the metal shack's wall.

Iris has used it before and offers to go first, 'Copy me'!

As she speaks, a vision comes into his mind. The XYZ Papini having heightened his senses, he can now see the androids waiting outside. Worse, he sees the Inspector from the port dragging a small bloodied and beaten Jerseyan, who spasms inside an Electrolock. It's Gs! It appears that he has succumbed to his torture and given up their location. If true, the Universal Council must also know that the trio seeks the Universal Council's base. Perhaps they shouldn't have shared this information, but they certainly can't turn back now. Strangely, the sirens' wailing ceases, VanWest knows something is about to happen.

In a low voice, VanWest informs them that 'they have Gs! We MUST go'.

An alarmed LeSouris finishes some more XYZ Papini before replying, 'We better transport then'!

A panicked Sista Cee pushes Iris out of her way as she runs towards the metallic wall, disappearing as a loud bang rocks the building. The walls glowing red, VanWest urges Iris to go. Doing well to stay aligned with the beam, she disappears after a short run. The room turns into a furnace, the Inspector trying to incinerate the walls to reach them. He grabs LeSouris and shoves him forward, unsteady on his feet after licking up more hyper Papini, he staggers along the line and disappears.

The Magicbox's laser beam starts to falter, smoke coming out from its side, short-circuiting after transporting three in quick succession. VanWest sprints towards the melting wall, hoping that the beam holds long enough for him to pass through.

Bang! The door breaks open with the next loud thug, followed by a volley of shots that ricochets along the, now empty, hallway. VanWest teleporting in the nick of time

Chapter 8 Eradication of Ellsworth and Queen Elizabeth

A moment never thought possible in the history of the Enforcers has arrived. After VanWest's rallying cry, Colonel Cornelius's death and Captain Kun-lee's victory over Master Jiang, the Enforcers have won a free vote to decide their future. Following a period of hesitation, the votes come in fast.

But it's not long until the Universal Council reacts. Not accepting any challenge to their authority, Commissioner Ming delivers an ominous message: *Effective Immediately The Space Soldiers Will Take Control Of Queen Elizabeth. Be Sure To Stand-down And Comply. All Those That Took Part In This Unauthorised Vote Have DEFIED The Commandments And ARE Considered TRAITORS.*

The news shocks all, but even for those yet to vote, their future looks bleak, 'the Space Soldiers will take control'. Effectively, they have all been made redundant and without purpose. For Enforcers, there has never been such a thing as retirement. With most dying before 30, their lives usually end in one of two ways, the first being killed in action and, for those less fortunate, the second being sent for 'rehabilitation' in Ward B of the moon base's medical complex. For all their 'privileges', their life expectancy mirrors more that of a citizen than an Elite. This status of 'Elite' and immortality ever so elusive.

With his hip wound patched, Captain Kun-lee sits up straight to show Dr VonHelmann the message. The Universal Council's harsh reaction has, in fact, worked in his and the EaR's favour. Even without the votes counted the Enforcers of Queen Elizabeth have been marked as 'enemies', by choice or not they are now on the same side.

A smiling, calculating Dr VonHelmann had hoped for this outcome, keen to press his advantage he seeks more than a ceasefire, he wants to make an official alliance. Addressing Colonel Mathieu, Captain Dell and Captain Kun-lee, he pressures, 'Look at what thy evil machines do now, they take thy role, thy purpose of existence. Join with us, forge an alliance with the NEA and Utopians. Join in the New Beginning'!

Albeit unsurprised by the Council's reaction, Captain Kun-lee feels slightly guilty, 'Never have I been a traitor. I only meant to uphold the Code of Honour'.

'I too have never betrayed', Captain Dell laments.

'This is not the time to dwell', Colonel Mathieu advises.

But Dr VonHelmann extols to them the merit of their new status as 'traitors', 'You are now free Enforcers, able to make thy own choices. Seize it'!

Colonel Mathieu decides it's time to declare, the Enforcers having overwhelmingly voted *1. Yes*. The Enforcers though are too stunned to react, having gathered in the courtyard they look to their leaders, the Captains and Colonel, for guidance.

But the Universal Council are first to take action, Colonel Mathieu hologram fades, and a message comes through, *Ellsworth UNDER ATTACK. Colonel Mason ATTACKS With 100 Enforcer patrolships. 10 Universal Spaceships.* A second message quickly follows, *Neurotoxins Released - Citizens Dying In The Streets.*

Enforcers of different settlements fighting one another - never has this happened before. As with the massacre of the citizens in ColaBeers, Colonel Mason proves yet again to be unscrupulous. Always Dr King's 'yes' man, he now seeks to kill Colonel Mathieu to become the Enforcer's one and only Colonel. Captain Kun-lee gets to his feet, he knows they must react. They MUST fight.

Dr VonHelmann continues, 'Name yourself Free Enforcers and join Earth's resistance, EaRA.... What say you? Do you trust? Do you embrace us'?

Pretoria brings more news, this time from New Jersey, showing all a short message from Warlord Method A, *PATH Broken. Universal Law. Chaos Coming To Journal Square Next. Help Us Land Peeps.*

'Commissioner Ming make attack on Ellsworth, attack on Jerseyans. Attack on all. We must unite'! Pretoria insists.

There is nowhere to run, they only have one choice; the captains, Kun-lee and Dell, nod to each other in agreement, much to Dr VonHelmann's delight. Captain Kun-lee answers solemnly, 'We are Free Enforcers, we support the EaRA'! He next replies to Colonel Mathieu's message, hoping it can still get past the Universal Council's jamming devices, *Queen Elizabeth Free Enforcers Come To Your Aid. So Come The NEA, Utopians. Together We Are Earth's Resistance.*

In front of all Enforcers, on the 4D holoscreens, the Captains, Dr VonHelmann and Pretoria extend their hands to seal their new alliance. They embrace the NEA way, gripping the hands and elbows of each other tightly. What this new alliance entails is still to be decided, but Dr VonHelmann already sees himself very much as its leader.

'We are Free Enforcers, we are EaRA'! Captain Kun-lee declares.

'Praise be'! Dr VonHelmann hails as he turns to the watching, now free, Enforcers. Without consulting the others, he pushes for even more, 'Enforcers, come Free Enforcers, let us go to Ellsworth, support Colonel Mathieu and defeat this coward, Colonel Mason... Onwards then to defeat Commissioner Ming. What say you'?

Captain Dell is the first to reply, 'Affirmative! I FREE Enforcer join you'!

In a lower voice, Captain Kun-lee says next, 'Affirmative, I Free Enforcer join'.

Prompting the other Enforcers to follow suit, one after the other, 'Affirmative! I Free Enforcer join'!

Antarctica's capital, Queen Elizabeth, houses by far the largest number of patrolships of any settlement, there too is an equal presence of NEA battleships. Just like with LeSouris's Hawkeye well-hidden throughout the capital. Together under the EaRA, their combined number reaches nearly 400 strong.

Captain Kun-lee stands straight to give his first order, 'Free Enforcers, follow Captain Dell to the armoury, equip and get ready. We go to Colonel Mathieu's aid'!

A blue-light flashes as the well-drilled Free Enforcers rush to assemble. Quick to put on their hazmat masks, in expectation of countering neurotoxins in Ellsworth's air. More used to taking orders, Captain Kun-lee now finds himself a decision-maker; his weariness and indecision are gone - he has evolved into a leader.

A new scrambled message comes through from Colonel Mathieu, *Retreated To HQ. 20 Patrol-lll-ships Remain-nnn. Queen Elizabeth Ne-xt-ttt.*

Judging by Colonel Mason's speed of action, he must have been busy organising the attack as the vote took place. Pretoria tries to reassure a stunned Captain Kun-lee that Colonel Mathieu can still be saved, 'Top pilot, Houston make way here with the NEA fleet, we make quick to Ellsworth'!

However, it is simply too late to help now. Dr VonHelmann purposely diverts their attention back to the capital and its defence, 'Let us establish control of Queen Elizabeth first and organise our forces, we don't want to be the ones caught by surprise next'.

Captain Kun-lee grimaces, he knows he is right, 'Affirmative'.

Almost on cue, a large number of NEA battleships decloak outside the forcefield, including the spirally and pointy ship of Houston 'The Star Fighter'. Being the NEA's best pilot, she ranks high in the Universal Council's *Most Wanted* list, her skill and experience will be most valuable. Captain Dell immediately signals to let her fleet through and to dock above the patrolship station, located not too far away from the courtyard.

Their arrival proves timely, 'Enemy ships'! As the battleships pass and the forcefield goes back up, the Enforcers sound the alarm.

Boom! Rays of intense red-light smack against the forcefield, temporarily blinding all those inside. The Space Army's Lt. Colonel Indium has joined Colonel Mason, adding a further 10 spaceships to the Colonel 150 patrolships. A former Universal Games winner, he brings great expertise and skill as well as formidable ships to this battle. This development does not bode well. Ellsworth likely having fallen, the EaRA must work hard to prevent the capital and its citizens sharing the same fate.

Captain Kun-lee marshals the Free Enforcers, he knows their forcefield will not last long, 'Sergeant Chang secure the perimeter north and east, Captain Dell go to the command centre to keep us informed of movements and help coordinate, affirmative'?

'Affirmative', Sergeant Chang and Captain Dell reply in unison.

Pointing at another sergeant he trusts in, he instructs, 'Sergeant Danu, south and west' perimeter.

'Affirmative'!

The gathered Free Enforcers and Sergeants split into two groups, to guard the perimeter.

Captain Dell immediately transports into the command centre and interfaces with the holomap to keep all updated. The enemy forces have moved to surround the HQ, ready to storm inside once the forcefield collapses.

Captain Dell advises all, 'Auxiliary defences activated. Guard towers manned... Prepare to engage'.

Being a skilled pilot, Kun-lee decides to lead the air defences, leaving Captain Dell to command the Enforcers on the ground. He salutes Dr VonHelmann and Pretoria before leaving.

Not skilled at flying, Pretoria offers his help to the Sergeants, 'Houston help in air, I help on ground'. Sergeant Danu accepts and hands him a Plasma blaster, offering him to join the defence of the north and east perimeter. In addition to battleships, there are NEA rebels close to Mid-City, Pretoria sends a message for them to come and support.

This will be the first test of the EaRA, an epic one at that, with the Free Enforcers, NEA and Utopians fighting together on the same side. On request, Houston flies over to transport Dr VonHelmann inside, the safest place for him to be at this moment. With the new alliance sealed, she sends an update to all contacts, 'Communicating on all channels, only attack Mason Enforcers and Space Soldiers, those outside of HQ'. No Enforcer inside the HQ will be attacked.

Boom! The forcefield continues to weaken. The majority of Colonel Mason's Enforcers come to the south and west side to commence the attack. Although, a number continue to wait on the north and east perimeter, alongside a small contingent of Space Soldiers.

Captain Dell advises, 'Forcefield down on next hit'!

'Power up, boys and girls'! Houston readies her fleet.

'Affirmative, ready to go', Captain Kun-lee does the same.

Boom! Upon the forcefield's collapse, Houston and Captain Kun-lee immediately counter. Their shields up, they are quick to attack Colonel Mason's patrolships, who take the brunt of the early exchange. Strangely, Lt. Colonel Indium's 10 spaceships stay further back, seemingly content to watch Colonel Mason enter the battle alone.

The Lt. Colonel's own spaceship is one of the newest and most advanced class, the MajorLasor series (MLS). The MLS-5 packs the firepower of 5 SCC class ships and 8 patrolships combined. Their engagement will be brutal for the EaRA if and when it comes. More worryingly, this small number of spaceships represent only a fraction of the entire Space Army's fleet. If VanWest, Iris and LeSouris cannot find and kill Dr King on Mars, battling an armada close to 90 times this size could be next.

With greater numbers, Houston and Captain Kun-lee overwhelm the first row of Mason's patrolships. Likely not having anticipated that the, now free, Enforcers of Queen Elizabeth would align with the NEA so quickly, Colonel Mason finds himself outgunned. From the command centre, Captain Dell updates all on the movements on the ground, 300 of Colonel Mason's Enforcers charge forward on the west perimeter.

Pretoria signals those NEA rebels that have arrived to engage. Well-versed in guerrilla warfare, they launch an attack of their own on the superiorly armed Mason Enforcers. They too wear protective hazmat masks, anticipating the release of neurotoxins. Many citizens and Utopians have also arrived at the HQ, amassing on the west side they come armed with a plethora of makeshift weapons, some only with metal poles and stones. Encouraged by the NEA engagement, they join the attack on Colonel Mason's Enforcers, who are forced to halt their advance on the HQ, as expected to release odious green gas neurotoxins to defend their rear guard.

Agh! Scores are slaughtered. Pretoria pleads for a reaction from Sergeant Danu, 'Make attack, make quick'! But, unlike in the skies, the coordination of their defence-is not so smooth.

Sergeant Danu stares at him, unable to accept his request, 'Do not copy that. Order to hold perimeter'.

Pretoria shakes his head, he yells at him, 'Citizen die! Make attack, make quick'!

Captain Dell doesn't respond either over the communicator. Instructed to defend the HQ, they are reluctant to expend Enforcer lives to save the citizens. Lives that in normal circumstances would be deemed not high enough in value.

Agh! The citizens' screams continue, the poison gas choking them. Despite this, many fervently continue to charge. Most are Utopians, *U* inked on their necks, they are willing to die for this next 'New Beginning' that Dr VonHelmann promises. The NEA rebels try to protect as many as they can but can do little.

An exasperated Pretoria implores the Free Enforcers once again to help, a frontal attack could save lives, 'Take fight to Mason, help on west side, make quick'!

With Captain Kun-lee engaged above, Captain Dell is the decision-maker. No longer able to watch, Pretoria shakes his head and charges. Skilfully ducking and diving, Pretoria rapidly advances and reaches the first squad of Mason's Enforcers, delivering a powerful blast from close range that ploughs through two. His act preventing this squad from releasing more neurotoxins.

It causes a reaction, Sergeant Danu, impressed by his brave act, contacts the command centre, 'Captain Dell, permission to charge, affirmative'?

After a long pause, Captain Dell finally agrees, 'Affirmative, engage on west side'!

Sergeant Danu signals all to 'charge'!

Seeing this, Mason Enforcers on the north and east side react too, markedly again without the Space Soldiers' support. Like in the skies, they stay back, only engaging the odd citizen that drifts over into their proximity. Sergeant Chang is easily able to repel the Mason Enforcers. Another danger emerges, the destruction of patrolships sends smouldering metal parts raining down. Making for a battleground reminiscent of the final stage of the Universal Games, the *Fires of Vesta* with its meteorite and debris fields.

Houston decides to make a run at Colonel Mason's Elite SCC class ship, SCC-100, 'Captain, you got my back? Going for leader'!

Working well together, Captain Kun-lee skilfully moves to cover, 'Affirmative! Roaching get him'! Captain Kun-lee directs his patrolships closest to her to join him in drawing attention away, commencing a series of daring flyby manoeuvres.

Colonel Mason takes the bait, expending a great deal of power to fire at the patrolships, Houston is able to swoop in and line up her shot. It comes spiralling through. *Boom!* Mason's crew unable to divert power back to the shields in time, the shot smacks into the command deck, causing a chain reaction that sweeps through - *kaboom*. The SCC-100 lighting up against the setting sun, this is a significant moment for the EaRA. They cheer through their communicators, Colonel Mason is dead!

'Yeeha'! Houston screams.

'Good shooting'! Captain Kun-lee salutes her.

However, their celebration is short-lived, Lt. Colonel Indium finally joins the fray, directing all his spaceships as well as his own MLS ship to focus on the unshielded command centre. Kun-lee tries to warn Captain Dell through his communicator, 'Get out! Quick'! But it is too late. The Lt. Colonel had laid his own trap and this time catches the EaRA by surprise.

In a split second, the command centre is obliterated with Captain Dell instantly pulverised. A thermal wave incinerating all the watchtowers, lashing at the feet of the units fighting at the outer perimeters. Few others are killed, but Captain Dell's death is a big blow. Captain Kun-lee is unable to contain his emotions and charges at the Lt. Colonel's much more formidable and advanced ship, 'This Space roach is mine'!

Now, Houston instructs her battleships to provide cover but, before Kun-lee can engage, a large Elite SCC ship decloaks and pulls in front of his patrolship. Strangely, its weapons are not pointed at him, rather at the MLS ship! It's the SCC-40, piloted by Lt. Colonel Wang, the Elite guard to the Hubert family, owners of numerous monopolies including InsectnOut and Demron.

Captain Kun-lee receives a message, *The Huberts And Lt. Colonel Wang Offer Support. Do You Accept?* He does not hesitate, sending a one-word reply, *YES*.

Despite the Huberts being part of the legacy of the Universal Council, Kun-lee knows this battle is at a critical juncture, he wants revenge, and the EaRA needs the Hubert's help. Kun-lee and Lt. Colonel Wang join together in firing at the impenetrable shield of Lt. Colonel Indium's MLS class spaceship. Not able to destroy it, they at least force him to divert all power to his shields and into retreat. One that instigates the withdrawal of the rest of his spaceships as well as Space Soldiers on the ground. With no care for Mason's Enforcers, they indiscriminately pound the settlement, hitting many as they do so.

On the north and east side, Sergeant Chang now instructs the Free Enforcers to charge out. Being hit on all sides, Mason's Enforcers fall like flies, their discipline failing, with some even trying to run away, but there is nowhere to go. Sergeant Chang shouts at them to 'get down' and 'surrender'! But it is worse than running, in normal times considered a dishonour and punishable by torture and execution, no Enforcer submits.

Further adding to the chaos, the few Space Soldiers that have been left behind start to beep, their detonation killing scores of Utopians and citizens that overwhelm their position. Sergeant Chang continues undeterred, coming face-to-face with the last few Mason Enforcers, he pulls out his laser sword. *Boom!* Another Space Soldier explodes close by. His armour not enough to protect against the intense heat, his laser sword is incinerated, his unprotected hands and face terribly burnt.

It marks the end of the battle and a first hard-fought victory for EaRA, their losses moderate with 140 patrolships and 150 battleships remaining active. Houston orders hers to trail Lt. Colonel Indium, whose small contingent now withdraws in the direction of New Jersey. The spaceships record no losses but have wilfully stood by as Mason's Enforcers were completely wiped out. It seems for the Universal Council that their mission was one of maximal damage rather than victory.

Houston returns Dr VonHelmann to the ground as she leaves, waving his arms in the air he joyfully greets the Utopians that now swarm the wrecked Enforcer HQ.

'Praise be to Utopia! Today we win a great battle for our New Beginning'!

They chant loudly, 'Trust in Utopia'!

The Free Enforcers and NEA rebels come together once more, this time to treat the injured, a badly burnt Sergeant Chang among them. Even though the capital lies in ruins, its fate is at least not that of Ellsworth. Grim news filtering through that the settlement has indeed been eradicated, hundreds of thousands of citizens slaughtered.

Leaving the chanting Utopians, Dr VonHelmann joins a tired Pretoria and Kun-lee in the courtyard, they need to organise their next steps. Lt. Colonel Wang requesting to join them, they take this respite to rehydrate with some water capsules.

'Praise be to Utopia, we have won the day'! Dr VonHelmann exclaims once again.

'Make great pride, Earth Resistance save Queen Elizabeth', Pretoria answers as they embrace the NEA way. Keen to bring their attention back to aiding the warlord Method A, of which there have been no more messages.

'Make next to Journal Square', Pretoria urges, knowing that Lt. Colonel Indium withdrew in that direction.

'Agree'! Captain Kun-lee has his own motives, revenging the death of Captain Dell and the other Free Enforcers. He wants to press home their advantage; if possible strike at and kill Commissioner Ming. Dr VonHelmann shares this motive too, his smile wide, he agrees.

Lt. Colonel Wang beams down and salutes them, he brings them the offer of his Elite services, 'Thank you for having me. The Huberts offer their SCC-40 and I to your cause, this in exchange for clemency. Do you accept'?

The Huberts dare to do what no other Elite has done, back the EaR to prevail. The others still deeming their likelihood of success too low. Having already accepted the help of Lt. Colonel Wang in the battle above, an intervention that likely saved his life, Captain Kun-lee agrees. Dr VonHelmann also does not hesitate to accept his offer, 'Let it be so. Praise be! I will join you on the SCC-40, a perfect base of operations'.

Pretoria, the NEA leader of Queen Elizabeth, is less forgiving, he has lost many rebels, friends, and felt first-hand the pain inflicted by the privileged Elites. But he is a rational, pragmatic man and decides not to challenge, 'Doctor make decision'.

The EaRA grows stronger, their next stop to come to the aid of the Method cousins in Journal Square, with the aim of once and for all ridding Earth of Commissioner Ming.

Chapter 9 The Mural in the Icy Chamber

On Mars, having transported via the Magicbox, VanWest finds himself lying on top of a bed of ice. His body transformed back to normal, the Jerseyan gills on his neck are gone, and his skin tone is no longer colourless. But not everything went perfectly, rematerialising between two large blocks of ice, his right arm is stuck, and he is unable to sit up straight. Iris is beside him, shivering and looking very puzzled. She is also fortunate to have arrived in one piece, having also transformed back to her human self.

Pitch-black, they are unable to see each other. Wherever they have arrived is extremely cold, perhaps as low as minus 25 degrees celsius. Struggling to breathe, Iris expends a great amount of energy to call out for 'LeSouris'. A murmur returns, indicating he's close by. He's alive but he's not quite the same, whilst his skin colour and pointy ears have returned, his neck still features the Jerseyan's fishlike gills. The Magicbox locking in some of his altered DNA as the teleportation took him here. Wherever here is!

'My word, this is terrible, my neck'? LeSouris whines as he crawls over, touching his neck with his cold hands. 'Do I have and you not'?

'Not', Iris replies.

Having managed to get to her feet, Iris tries her best to help VanWest to get his arm unstuck. However, the ice burns her skin - too cold to touch with her bare hands. While the Magicbox did its job in transporting them out of the trading post, it's a mystery as to where they have arrived. With their tech not fully working, likely due to the extreme cold, this place seems to be an icy, rocky prison. They are at a loss on what to do.

VanWest notices that Sista Cee is not with them and asks, his teeth clattering, 'Sista Cee... Cee'?

LeSouris and Iris also call out 'Sista Cee', but nothing returns. Braving the cold, Iris treads a few meters forward and calls once again 'Sista', only for one of her boots to become stuck in something sticky. She bends down to inspect, only to find her emerald ring embedded in an icy puddle of goo. It takes a moment before it dawns on her, she stumbles backwards and lets out a low, long shriek - *agh*!

Her eyes too cold to cry, she returns, 'She is... goo-oo'!

'My word'! LeSouris replies. Thinking to himself that he is now not so unfortunate to have Jerseyan the gills after all he's at least alive.

LeSouris inspects the goo to confirm, pulling the ring from the sticky, icy puddle to return it to a shaken Iris, 'Your ring, yes'?

Iris replies, her teeth clatter, 'Yes, afraid so... poor Jerseyan'.

This being Mars, the chamber is also filled with dry ice, burning on touch it is made up of carbon dioxide. VanWest is lucky to have his jumpsuit under his Jerseyan rags; otherwise, he would have suffered severe burns. But he can feel his body succumbing to the cold. He needs to get out.

Sliding her ring back on her finger, she is surprised to find that it is oddly warm. 'Whoa'! It then begins to glow, soon so bright that it illuminates everything around them. The light revealing a large chamber decorated with icicles; its ice hides numerous and intricate rock drawings, mostly those of men, women and children, staring upwards. Seemingly, to a ledge that hangs over them.

'This is no random place', VanWest cryptically states in a low voice. He feels drawn to the ledge, he must go there. The ring triggers the icicles to begin melting, so much so that they are forced to cover their heads as they fall all around. VanWest is now able to wriggle free and embraces Iris with a big hug. The warmth helping his frozen body to sit up.

Amazed by what he sees, LeSouris is also drawn to the ledge, and enthusiastically urges them to go up there, 'My friends, praise be! We climb up to this ledge, yes'?

VanWest somehow knows this to be a holy place, the drawings depictions of Martians, his origins. He surmises that it cannot be a coincidence that they have all arrived here, and with Sista Cee in a gooey puddle this was unlikely her intended destination.

'Yes, this is no random place. We come here for a reason, we must go up there'.

'What do you mean this is no random place'? Iris asks, only for VanWest to shake his head, unable to answer at this moment.

LeSouris points to well-trodden stepping stones, shoeprints of varying sizes clearly visible, that go to this ledge. Spaced far apart, each will require a perfectly balanced leap to get from one to another. For VanWest's long legs, this is a rather straightforward climb, and he proceeds at pace. LeSouris and Iris follow, trying to match his athleticism, only to find each jump harder than the one before.

As VanWest reaches and hops onto the ledge, his heavy foot causes a large sheet of ice to fall down in front. Revealing a most amazing sight, a wall full of precious and colourful stones, on closer inspection, a splendid mural. VanWest is instantly transfixed, his mind euphoric. The ornate square stones of the mural have been arranged in the form of a garden, with colourful pink and yellow flowers interspersed between green shrubs that encircle a large bluish-greenish lake or pond. It must be a depiction of Mars centuries ago. Dr VonHelmann had told him that this world was once green and rich, Utopian like.

An inscription illuminates, in the bottom corner, *Bewakers van de Groene Utopie*, translating to Guardians of a Green Utopia. Dutch the old language of its first colonisers, the language remained in use for official texts and ceremonies, with English being its main spoken language. Indeed, the name of the Martian's last President, his namesake and clone source Dederic Van der Westhuizen, is of Dutch heritage too.

LeSouris follows VanWest and hops onto the ledge, not quite as agile and in shape, it proves more difficult to reach. After taking a moment to balance, his eyes too becomes transfixed as he looks over, marvelled by the mural's exquisiteness and mystery, 'It cannot be! I heard tales but my word... Mars looked like this mural? Green with vegetation. Praise Utopia'!

VanWest looks curiously at him, 'Tales'? He wants to know more.

LeSouris pats him on the back, his knowledge coming from Dr VonHelmann as well, 'Yes, my friend. Doctor tell me people lived on Mars. The place not simply sand and dirt'. Pointing at the inscription, 'This was Groene Utopie'!

'Ah, he told me the same', VanWest replies. He actually knows more, that Dr VonHelmann came to Mars as an interplanetary official, diplomat of the then Grand Council, before its destruction and genocide of its Martian inhabitants.

Iris arrives last, VanWest stretches over to help her from the last stepping stone and onto the ledge. Just like with VanWest and LeSouris, she too becomes instantly transfixed. But, with a keen eye for detail, immediately notices a couple of irregularities. There are two missing pieces, a circular one from what appears to be a large flower or sun, yellowish-orange in colour, and another from the bluish-green lake. Her ring glows brighter as she brings her hand closer, in fact so bright they all squint. The chamber's new warmth originating from this mural, its energy has been triggered.

Yet more astonishing, her ring's emerald is similar in size and colour as the lake's missing piece. This cannot be yet another coincidence!

'Your ring, where did you get it. From your father, right'? VanWest probes.

'Yes... Papa gave it to me', Iris answers.

'And how did he get it'? VanWest says in an accusative tone.

'I do not know. He always said it came from a faraway place, seeing this I guess it came from Mars'.

'Faraway? How far exactly'?

Iris doesn't like VanWest's tone, replies sarcastically, 'Maybe he stole it'!

She takes off her ring and hands it to him, 'Have it! Figure out what it means'!

LeSouris suggests, 'My friends, calm down... Try to bring it closer'.

Taking hold of the ring, he moves the emerald closer to the missing piece in the bluish-green lake to see if it causes any additional reaction. Pulling at him, the emerald turns not only brighter but also much bluer. *Creak!* He steps back as a sharp noise grows.

'Duck'! A large ice stalagmite breaks off and drops onto the ledge. The chamber shakes, the rocks below shifting and causing even more icicles to fall. Warming up, the melting accelerates, and the dry ice blocks sublimate away.

Swoosh! The water spirals as it drains from the chamber, creating a most stupendous and surreal scene. The emerald a key, which brought close to the mural has triggered a mechanism. They huddle together, not knowing what comes next as the icy water drains completely from the chamber.

La-la-la!

'Do you hear the sweet song'? VanWest asks. But LeSouris and Iris shake their heads, they cannot.

La-la-la!

He turns back to look at the mural and freezes! There's a little girl that glowers at him, her eyes dark green, it is the same girl from his earlier vision, that of Van der Westhuizen's memory. In her ghostly hands, there's the other missing piece from the mural, which he recognises to be the same orange-yellowish stone her father gave her.

The girl's eyes narrow as she yells in a high-pitched voice, 'Papie, you killed us'!

A startled VanWest stumbles backwards, fortunate to bump into LeSouris, who saves him from falling off the ledge.

‘Careful, my friend. You ok? You look like you seen a ghost’? LeSouris looks at VanWest with concern, as does Iris who comes over and puts her hand on his shoulder. As they do, the girl disappears, fading into the mural.

‘You didn’t see her’? VanWest asks in a shrill voice.

‘See who’? LeSouris replies. Already alarmed by the draining of the water, ‘My word, I think this place is too much, no’?

With the ice gone, they find more writing etched into the rock beside the mural, though this one is much rougher and coarser than the rest. ‘Ah’! As they step forward to read, they make another startling discovery. This one most grim, that of a cadaver wedged in a divot between the mural and ledge.

Noting the same white jumpsuit that he saw President Van der Westhuizen wear in his vision, VanWest immediately identifies it to be ‘Martian’! Lying beside is a metal stencil. He had etched into the rock, a hard to decipher message in English:

Our Land. Our People - No More.
Our Stone. Our Energy. Our Gift - Betrayed.
All Gone. No Survivors. No Women. No Children.
The Evil Desires. All Our Resources.
Our Niobium. Our Polar Ice. To Cool their Nuclear Ships.
Our Utopie Gone - We Are No More.

Despite the tragic writing, LeSouris cannot help but feel excited, this mural a further confirmation than Groene Utopie existed. It is, or was, here on this planet, ‘My friends, praise be! Maybe the answer lies here to restore Utopia, this mural a key. Utopia not lost after all, but here on Mars all along’!

With the Utopian mission to change the past having failed, LeSouris is hopeful that Utopia can still be found. VanWest is also intrigued, particularly by *Our Stone*, he wonders if this is the same as the girl’s. Trying to piece together all he has seen, the church and this seems all to be related to *Our Energy*. LeSouris could be right: this stone is a key. Recalling Dr VonHelmann’s interface, he wonders if the stone was how the Council's forces got through Mars's impenetrable shield.

VanWest turns to Iris to get her opinion, only to find her in tears. Unlike LeSouris, her first thought is not of rejoicing at the possibility of finding Utopia. Rather a sense of deep sadness for the Martians, their population wiped out, made extinct. VanWest puts a comforting arm around her and gives a gentle kiss on her forehead.

Not pleased with LeSouris, she replies pointedly, 'Perhaps Utopia is here... Let us not forget ourselves, let us take a moment to pay our respects. These poor souls'.

'Poor souls, indeed', VanWest joins in a moment of silence.

'Yes, of course. Meant no disrespect', LeSouris agrees.

The moment passing, Iris thoughts turn to the motive behind their deaths, 'Niobium, a rare-earth metal used in Superconductors. The evil Council needed this to power their ships. Their deaths... pure greed'.

VanWest confirms, 'My sweet, yes, your father showed me this, this the cause of the genocide'. As the Space Army and Dr King now prepare to repeat history on Earth's citizens.

La-la-la!

As he finishes speaking, he notices that the sweet sound has returned. VanWest turns slowly to find the little girl gazing up at him once more, this time she no longer appears angry, instead she is playful and skips along the ledge. LeSouris and Iris still do not see or hear her; instead; they discuss how to exit from this chamber.

VanWest walks up to the girl and crouches down beside her, whispering in her ear, not quite sure who to address her as, 'I'm sorry. I, he, didn't mean to kill you. He couldn't foresee this evil. Forgive me, us. I need your help to make amends'.

Recognising him as her father, she smiles back and puts her ghostly hand over his, sending a tingling, warm feeling through him that jolts his mind forward in time. He sees a lab and the swarmy and bearded face of Dr Minus Schuurman. The snake-like

Interrogator and the near cyclops-eyed Commissioner Ming are there too, laughing at a badly tortured and beaten Gs, his colourless skin burnt a bright red. But something quite bizarre comes into view; VanWest sees someone that looks remarkably like himself, half-naked he carries a tray of drinks and wears a medical bib.

VanWest wants to call out, but the vision changes, the scene becoming even more surreal and horrifying. Dr Schuurman stands bare-chested with an odd-looking dagger, wearing a blue and green featured headdress. Under him is a naked man tied to a flat rock, a round stone sermon. Unable to see more, VanWest moves his hand away, breaking the vision.

The little girl begins to fade, walking to the edge of the ledge, she whispers, 'The church', before jumping. VanWest tries to catch her, but her ghostly body passes through his hands as she disappears.

Noticing his strange behaviour, Iris grabs his arm and shakes him, very worried she asks him in succession, 'What are you doing? Why are you talking to yourself? Are you feeling ok'?

VanWest recomposes himself and gives Iris a reassuring hug, doing his best to look ok. The whole vision quite unnerving, he is most of all shocked to see himself serving drinks to these evil men. Horrified to think this could be showing his fate. Colonel Cornelius's last words replaying in his mind, warning him to 'beware yourself'. Still, he feels a presence compelling him on - that he must go and confront whatever is fated.

VanWest notices that his tech works again, he wastes no time in accessing the Colonel's red chip to search for his location as well as the hidden base. Whilst the chamber they stand-in is not marked, he is relieved to find that they have arrived in the Alba Mons mountain range, his Moggle X map showing a symbol of a small peak on top. But as he zooms in, a voice calls in his mind, 'VanWest'! It is not quite his own.

Iris takes his hand and points to a possible exit, the spot where the icy water drained, 'My love, you see it'.

'Yes, my sweet. My Moggle X places us close to Alba Mons', VanWest reveals.

LeSouris takes this as another great sign, 'Praise be'! He asks again more detail, 'My friend, the plan'?

Again, VanWest is unable to articulate it, 'Like you say, we must trust'!

Seeing VanWest's weariness, Iris recommends they rest up before trekking further, 'Let's get some sleep. We need to gather our strength for what lies ahead, a couple of hours won't hurt'.

LeSouris agrees, replying with a smile, 'Our mission, our destiny can wait a little longer'!

Having carried with her some energy pills, she distributes one to each. The trio lies down together on the ledge. VanWest though is unable to sleep, his mind continues to race. The voice calling, he stares at where the water drained - wondering what comes next. What is fated?

Chapter 10 Universal Law

'Warning Universal law in place, must comply'.

The situation in New Jersey is fraught. With the breaking of the PATH agreement made between the Universal Council and its four warlords: Method A, Method Bee, Rulez Haah, and Gangs Hater. Commissioner Ming now pushes deeper into Jerseyan territory, transporting on the top of the Transportation Center, close to Journal Square station, he comes to exert control here next. Accompanying him is Major Chromes, the prominent red team Space Soldier that nearly bested VanWest during the final stage of the Universal Games, critically wounding his squad member, Captain Barys, in the process.

Even though the Commissioner still seeks VanWest, his focus has switched to establishing 'Universal law' over New Jersey. The Universal Council commandments now fully apply:

1. *To serve without question the Universal Council*
2. *To work for the progression of man and the Universal*
3. *To destroy all those who defy the Universal Council*

No longer affording New Jersey the special privilege of anonymity. It makes for a ballsy move in troubled times, but Dr King commands a clampdown on all habited areas, and that means here too. The 'peeps', Jerseyans of Journal Square, arm themselves ready to react on Rulez Haah's instruction. Unfortunately, she herself does not fully realise the threat despite warnings coming from Harrison and Newark, the 'exit' of New Jersey's subway system. Having dismissed it as a problem exclusive to the Method cousins.

Her shocked looking guard, Bruva Lem, waits for Rulez Haah, the warlord of the east side of New Jersey, to give an answer on the Commissioner's message, including his condition to immediately handover both cousins.

'Commissioner says he will shoot us, must comply'!

The cousins look pensively at Rulez Haah, worrying that she too will allow the PATH agreement to be broken and side with the Universal Council, just as the warlord of Manhattan, Gangs Hater, has already done so. Another guard brings news that his fighters have amassed on the edge of her territory, 'Gangs edging into east side', outside Hoboken station and Exchange Place station.

'WHAT'? A visibly angered and surprised Rulez Haah yells. She readies to leave the room immediately, instructing her guards to 'get cousins ready', to meet the Commissioner and talk reason, 'Me go, strike deal'!

Knowing well the Commissioner's guile, Bee tries to warn her, 'Rulez, I go with. Commissioner is trickster, gonna try to play you, cheat you'.

'Zip it'! Rulez Haah doesn't want to hear him out; instead, she now instructs her guards to point their Electrozappers at each. Method Bee and Method A know how serious the situation is after their recent encounters with the Space Soldiers. They know too that she is too late to 'strike deal'. For the Commissioner has already picked his puppet ruler, Gangs Hater, hence his move to the edge of her territory.

Undeterred by the Electrozappers, Method A steps behind her, 'Commissioner offers Gangs Hater to be one and only warlord, you get me'?

Rulez Haah turns sharply and glowers at her, 'Nah, this is all because you helped that Enforcer, Captain VanWest. Why you meddle with land maggots? Been playing with the maggots for years, putting us all in danger. It's payback time, aye'!

'What you mean'? Method A barks back. But she knows there is an element of truth to this. Sooner or later, it was bound to catch up with her.

'I know... about your smuggling. Your contacts easy to sway with my moolah'.

Method A replies strongly, 'Silly dawg, you not get me. Gangs Hater make deal with Universal, now too late! They come to kill'!

Rulez Haah shakes her head, responding, 'Don't insult me. You not my family, you not my ally, why I gotta trust you'?

She is right. The Method cousins exchange a tense look, they know that they need a good answer, something to persuade her and save them all. If they can't, then they will all soon be dead, and with it what remains of the PATH, New Jersey and New York fully under the control of the Universal Council, under their puppet warlord Gangs Hater. They know full well how Antarctica and its citizens live. Virtually enslaved, their lives one of servitude, where simple freedoms do not exist, such as walking the street free from the harassment of Quadrotors. The right to travel to other planets and have a different viewpoint, among many others.

For all of New Jersey's weaknesses, they at least do not have dramatic inequalities. In New Jersey, warlords and normal 'peeps' don't live so differently. Albeit Rulez Haah's quarters are more opulent than most, this still pales in comparison to the Oligarchs, the Elites and their descendants. In this underground world, one can still make themselves a success, be it a cargo ship pilot, Papini farmer, casino boss or otherwise. Life is not so predefined.

Knowing her desire for him and his territory, a desperate Method Bee blurts out an audacious offer, 'We, we wed'! The room falls silent as he clarifies his offer to Rulez Haah, 'I become yours... Aye? Harrison part of your territory, we family'?

This is quite the sacrifice, as Jerseyan custom commands, becoming a husband abdicates his role of warlord. In so doing, Newark and Newark Penn station would become the only place in New Jersey not controlled by Rulez Haah, Method A the only other warlord. Initially taken aback, Rulez Haah smiles widely, the deal pleases her. Her pointy, gold and silver, teeth showing.

Rulez Haah sends Bruva Lem to stall the Commissioner, 'Go meet them, tell them I will come. Keep him busy, aye'!

Unfortunately, she is still not persuaded that there is no deal to be struck, but Method Bee has at least stopped her from taking them all to their deaths, at least for now. Rulez Haah beckons for her dancers to make their marriage official.

With clouds of multi-coloured powder thrown into the air, she looks happily into Method Bee's eyes and accepts his proposal, 'Make Rulez happy dawg, our bond sealed... The Methods make family, and I protect you'.

The two exchange a shaka sign of respect and she leans in to seal their union with the tips of their tongues rolling out and gently touching. Not a monogamous culture, Method Bee becomes the first of what could be many husbands. Effectively making Turnpike no longer a no-man's-land, the Jerseyan territory now split along the PATH network as follows:

- *Newark Penn 'The Exit' - Method A - Occupied by the Commissioner*
- *Harrison to Exchange Place and Hoboken - Rulez Haah*
- *Christopher Street, World Trade Center - Gangs Hater*

Calling to an end this warm moment, Method A repeats her call for Rulez Haah to react, 'We celebrate this great day later, aye! Right now, we gotta stop Space Soldiers, use cannons against their spaceships, aye'?

'Nah-nah... You gotta chill. Bee safe with me', Rulez Haah replies. Her viewpoint unchanged, she at least gives Method Bee her protection. He's no longer a warlord.

Bruva Lem notifies them, *Commissioner Meet On Rooftop, No Longer Stall Aye. Getting Hot.*

Rulez Haah makes her decision, 'Go armed. We meet them. My word is final, aye'! Making it clear that she will lead discussions.

Her guards gesture for Method A and Bee to follow, walking behind Rulez Haah as she leaves the chamber. Method A ponders what to do next, her last one-to-one encounter with Commissioner Ming ending with a head-butt to his chin, she knows he will not forgive and forget. She knows she MUST take the first opportunity she gets to save them both. And not allow Rulez Haah's willful ignorance to cost them their lives.

This time without the palanquin and her burgundy veil, Rulez Haah leads them back to the concrete flights of stairs and upwards until they reach the surface level, the ground reverberates even more strongly here. Still scantily dressed with her layers of wrinkled skin showing, she readies to greet the Commissioner. A worried-looking Bruva Lem waits on the stairs to the roof of the Transportation Center, like the Method cousins he also has misgivings.

Bruva Lem advises, 'My boss, I don't trust. Commissioner bad dawg'.

But Rulez Haah dismisses him as well, 'Bruva, zip it'!

Pushing past, she proceeds to the rooftop. Opening the large reinforced metal door, *EXIT*, she walks through to be met by the sight of the cyclops-eyed Commissioner in his black peak cap. Forebodingly, surrounding him are a hundred grey-skinned, red-eyed Space Soldiers. They all look identical, mechanically surveying for the heat signatures of the Jerseyan fighters hidden in the ruins around. Their towering presence, over six-foot-five meters tall, making them even more intimidating. The symbol *Cr* the only item identifying their tactical assault commander, Major Chromes.

Thump! In unison, they take one step forward as Rulez Haah slowly walks over. Slightly fazed by their might, she glances briefly back at Bruva Lem and her new husband, Method Bee, however, her only option is to proceed now. Convincing herself yet again that she can strike a deal with the Commissioner. Method A hangs back, keeping one eye on her cousin and one on the Space Soldiers. Major Chromes scans her, ready to engage - his weapon active.

'Commissioner, how can I help you'? Rulez Haah presents herself, trying her best to sound eloquent and compliant. But, as she speaks, there's another thump, the Space Soldiers step forward once more, moving closer to her.

'The warlords, Method A and Method Bee, hand them over', the Commissioner demands.

Rulez Haah takes a step back, as if having just realised her own naivety, and replies in a squeaky voice, 'Method Bee no longer warlord, my husband'. Seeing his threatening demeanour, 'I give you Method A. We deal? Aye'?

Method Bee gasps, 'You betray my cousin! We family'!

But as Rulez Haah looks back to answer, Bruva Lem screams, 'Watch out'!

Zap! The Commissioner removes out a small diamond phaser and fires it point-blank into Rulez Haah, the shot tearing through her torso. Without even a scream, she slumps to the floor as the Space Soldiers fire on the rest of the Jerseyans - *boom!*

Method A grabs her stunned cousin, as Bruva Lem and Rulez Haah's guards return fire. Major Chromes looks to strike her, only for the Jerseyan fighters scattered in the ruins to come to their aid, the ensuing deadly firefight lighting up the dark, cloudy sky. Like in Gambler's Den, the Electrozappers do little to slow the Space Soldiers, but it buys the Method Cousins just enough time to retreat.

Agh! Unable to reach his boss, Bruva Lem is forced to flee, only to be struck in his leg as he reaches the exit door. Method A and Bee come to his aid, dragging him inside and down the stairs. His near colourless, slightly bluish blood staining the floor. With all the guards on the roof neutralised, they bolt the door shut.

More Jerseyans fighters race up to defend their position. Among them is a 'medicine bruva', who is quick to rub a medicinal fungi gel on Bruva Lem's wound to staunch the bleeding, but he has been mortally wounded.

Boom! Shots fire into the reinforced metal door. Bruva Lem then grabs Method A's arm, announcing, 'With Rulez Haah dead, you boss here'. Bruva Lem's last act to block this entry point, 'Go now, I blow up stairway'.

With Method Bee having abdicated his status, she becomes the warlord of all of New Jersey. In a short amount of time, there becomes only two warlords: Gangs Hater and Method A.

'Bruva, much respect... You gonna feast well in great hall', Method A replies in a sad and squeaking voice, putting up a hang loose, shaka sign of respect, before leaving with Method Bee.

In no doubt that his courageous death will earn him a seat in the Chamber of Warriors. A Jerseyan belief that those who die in battle receive the ultimate honour of transcending to a great hall, lined with Papini of every flavour. Celebrating in a never-ending festival of music and feasting. An afterlife that promises to be better than this underground, hostile world.

Chapter 11 Journal Square Under Attack

Kaboom! Using the Space Soldier's trick against them, Bruva Lem blows himself up and seals the rooftop entrance.

With the news spreading of Method A becoming the new warlord, she wastes no time to address the Jerseyans of Journal Square, communicating to all, 'We not gonna let them go underground, we gotta fight them'! After their experience in Harrison, she warns next, 'Back away when those soldiers start beeping', their explosion most deadly.

She divides up the guards to defend the two-remaining ground-level entry points into the Transportation Center and the subway system from above, via John F Kennedy Boulevard and Summit Avenue. Although the station is well fortified, it is not designed to keep out the Space Army. Rulez Haah's slow reaction has left the east side of New Jersey ill-prepared.

Method A turns to Bee, intel suggesting John F Kennedy cannot withstand the assault, 'I gotta go to Boulevard'.

Method Bee has reservations, he thinks they should stick together at the subway entrance, 'Cousin, nah, nah'!

'No choice, Bee. Soldiers coming'!

Heeding her call, Jerseyans of all walks of life hurry up from the ground with makeshift weapons in hand; teenagers, mothers, fathers and elders all fighting together. Rulez Haah's personal guards no longer the only ones defending their home.

Boom! Shots ricochet along the concrete walls as Method A commands a dozen fighters to follow her into a corridor strewn with bodies of dead and injured guards. The grenades and missiles having created plumes of dust, they struggle to see ahead. More worryingly, there's also a whiff of noxious gas, just like that released in Ellsworth and Queen Elizabeth. Albeit the Jerseyans, with their layers of wrinkled skin are more resistant than humans, it risks eventually killing them if they are exposed too long.

A dying guard grabs her leg as she proceeds, warning that 'they storm past'.

If true, not only have the Space Soldiers taken the 'Boulevard', but they are inside. With not a second to lose, Method A signals all to scramble back to the subway entrance, 'Run NOW'. They risk being cut-off with nowhere to retreat, not even underground.

As she turns, the infamous Major Chromes walks through the dust, his plasma blaster pointing in their direction. *Bang!* He fires at the now-dead sista, knocking her head clean off her body, which rolls over to a shocked Method A. More Space Soldiers join Major Chromes, firing their weapons next. Method A rounds a corner as quickly as possible to get away. *Bang!* As another shot forces her to slide under a rusty metal table.

A short, fragmented message breaks through the Universal jamming devices, it is her contact from the World Trade Center subway stop in Manhattan, a cargo bay manager named Keys: *We-st At-ack.*

Not unexpected news, Gangs Hater begins his incursion of New Jersey's east side: Exchange Place and Hoboken. Not only has he allowed the PATH agreement to be broken and betrayed his own kind, he now kills fellow Jerseyans on behalf of the Universal Council. The Commissioner's offer to govern all of New Jersey as a puppet state, under him one puppet warlord, enough to sway him. The situation looks even bleaker for Method A and the Jerseyans.

Agh! The Space Soldiers continue to press, her Jerseyan fighters mowed down one after the other as they continue to fall back to Method Bee's position. Another blast throws the rusty table and Method A back. Her ears ringing, she is just about able to get to her feet. Narrowly missing the next wave of shots.

Thump! Rounding a second corner, a Space Soldier cuts her off, knocking her to the floor and her weapon away. All looks lost, but through a small crack in the wall, a king scorpion emerges, it's Ken! Having sensed the danger, he has followed from Turnpike to come to Method A's rescue. He clamps onto the Space Soldier and bends one of its elongated limps, his stinger following and blinding the Soldier, who immediately starts to beep. Method A grabs Ken's claw, pulling them just about far enough away before the Space Soldier stops beeping.

Kaboom! The ceiling caves in and flames lash at them. Just about making it back to the subway entrance, Method A is relieved to find a much-stressed Method Bee still holding the position.

'Crazy A! Get behind me'!

The noxious gas smell is strong here, an assault soon to follow. In addition to Ken, over 500 king scorpions have gathered on the stairs. The PATH network their home too, they come to defend it. Many others are fighting up and down the subway system to protect it from these intruders. The fight still raging in Harrison. Method Bee embraces Method A with a chest bump, relieved she has come back alive. His forehead though is even more wrinkled than usual, he knows they MUST act or risk opening up another entrance to the tunnels below. Already pressured from attacks east and west, New Jersey will be lost if they lose this position.

Method A rechecks her messages. Hoping for a reply from her NEA contact, rebel leader Pretoria, on her earlier request for support but there is none. Method Bee hands her cousin a new weapon, a Subway Hunter rifle. Alongside the king scorpions, a thousand more Jerseyans have also come. This they know a fight for their lives and livelihoods.

With these reinforcements, Method A returns to her plan, first to push the Space Soldiers out of the Transportation Center and second to relieve pressure on the aerial defences, so that they can challenge the spaceships in the skies. Whilst the numbers of Space Soldiers is far lower, they are superiorly armed and much stronger. To help give them extra resistance to the noxious gases, Rulez

Haah's servants hurry up and down the stairway, carrying plates and bowls of Papini powder.

Boom! Shots fire through the clouds of dust at their entrenched position. It's time. Method A waits for each to finish ingesting the Papini before giving the signal to charge.

'Bruvas and sistas, we go fight'. Lifting her weapon high, her look resolute, 'We gonna get revenge, for Journal, Rulez Haah, aye'!

'Aye'! The gathered fighters reply together. Their resolve is stronger than ever, they call out, 'For Rulez Haah! For Journal'!

Ken commences the counter with the king scorpions, who scurry through the cracks in the walls to launch a surprise attack on the Space Soldiers, latching onto their metallic limbs they pull them to the floor. Their attention diverted, Method A leads the Jerseyans forward through the noxious gas, firing in quick succession.

Major Chromes retreats behind the first row, keeping himself away from danger. Seeing the Space Soldiers greatly outnumbered, he orders a tactical retreat. Firing his Plasma blaster into the ceiling, he buries those at the front so the rest can get away.

Beep-Beep! A familiar sound returns.

Method A calls out to take shelter, 'Get back! Get down'!

Kaboom! The explosion spreads through, decimating everything in its path. Now aware of this danger, most take cover on hearing the sound. And Method A wastes no time in capitalising on the Space Soldiers retreat, splitting the Jerseyan fighters and king scorpions into two groups, hers to continue to Summit Avenue on the west side of the building and Method Bee the others to retake John F Kennedy Boulevard. Hoping to rid the surface of any remaining Space Soldiers as well as their tactical assault commander, Major Chromes.

Method A checks her communicator again for news from Pretoria, she is both relieved and excited to find his response: *Following Lt. Colonel Indium Spaceships. Earth Resistance, NEA, Free Enforcer Come To New Jersey To Expel Commissioner and Space Army.*

The EaRA does not so much come for altruistic reasons - to aid the Method cousins, they come to rid Earth of Commissioner Ming and the smaller contingent of the Space Army to prevent their return to the capital, this time supported by Gangs Hater's up-armoured cargo ships. Their speed of action critical. The Commissioner's heavy-handed approach to finding VanWest, including declaring Universal law in New Jersey, has left his forces stretched and allowed the NEA, Utopians and Free Enforcers to forge an alliance.

Notwithstanding, this small contingent has managed to kill so many in Antarctica and New Jersey. It's terrifying to think what the entire Space Army could do. The need for VanWest, Iris and LeSouris to find and kill Dr King remains vital to the defence of Earth.

Method A receives a second message from Pretoria, now closer the EaRA is able to circumvent the Universal's jamming devices: *Incoming 5 Min. Make Support.*

With this news of their imminent arrival, Method A sends a communication on all frequencies to continue the fight, 'Fire at them ships'.

Calling on any Jerseyan that can help. Those of her cargo ships not yet impounded or destroyed, emerge up-armoured, their shields at maximum join the fray as Method Bee updates that 'Boulevard clear, machines on the run'.

Zoom! But without warning, an intense red light fills the ground in and around Journal Square, blinding Method A and all the Jerseyans with her. In that instant, she finally realises the more sinister reason why Major Chromes retreated so quickly. It was a little too easy. Commissioner Ming has a lone MLS-Arts at his disposal, the most advanced long-range spaceship ever produced, from space it can hit any target on Earth with pinpoint accuracy. Lt. Colonel Indium, having withdrawn from Queen Elizabeth, also arrives. Universal's spaceships number as follows:

- *Commissioner Ming - SCC-300*
- *Major Chromes - MLS-25*

- *Lt. Colonel Indium - MLS-5*
- *20 Standard class spaceships*
- *MLS-Arts long-distance artillery spaceship*

Agh! The temperature soars, causing the stones around to heat up rapidly and redden. Method A collapses, she can see her skin boiling. A new message reads *30 Seconds*. She wonders if it is already too late for her. Looking around, the other Jerseyans are collapsing too, they do not have long until they are next to fall prey to the Space Soldiers' trickery.

Boom! The ground shakes violently, and the intense red light fades. Houston leads the battleships, Pretoria having joined her. Her fleet now numbers 250 strong, with more having joined from space and other areas of Earth. Trailing close behind is Captain Kun-lee, the commander of the Free Enforcers, leading the patrolships whose numbers also reach 250 strong. Dr VonHelmann and Lt. Colonel Wang come too, trailing further behind on the Elite SCC-40.

Albeit the spaceships are more advanced, they are far outnumbered by the combined fleets of the NEA, Free Enforcers and Method A's Jerseyans. Having already inflicted major damage and casualties, the Commissioner is not willing to put his own life at risk and immediately orders to withdraw and regroup on the red planet with Dr King. He knows that the Space Army commanded by Four-star General Vladimir will far outmatch the EaRA's eclectic fleet of 500 plus.

The melees have come at a steep cost to the Free Enforcers, losing half of their numbers, so too that of the NEA and nearly all of New Jersey's cargo ships. The battles over New Jersey and Queen Elizabeth may have been won, but the war is far from over.

The MLS-Art spaceship finally withdraws too, its damage has been huge, firing deep into the ground it has killed tens of thousands around Journal. Major Chromes leaves in his own MLS class ship, having transported the remaining Space Soldiers inside, they all speed to Mars. Less than two days travel away, one for the fastest spaceships.

'Method Bee, cousin, you good'? Method A asks through her communicator. But there is no answer, she asks again, 'Method Bee'!

Her skin still red, her mycelium clothing and shoes charred, she hurries to the other side of the Transportation Center, to John F Kennedy Boulevard. The damage here is much worse, most of the Jerseyans dead or dying. Rulez Haah's dancers rush to give those still breathing mushroom water to rehydrate and calm their wounds. Method A reaches Method Bee's last known position. Looking left and right desperately, she soon finds Method Bee, recognising a tattoo on his shoulder; that of a king scorpion - its once-mighty stinger with two large front claws has faded, partly melted along with his skin.

Method A kneels down beside, his body too hot to touch, his eyes white and milky he is barely able to speak.

'That you, A'?

'Yeah, Bee. I gonna get you out of here'.

'The jig is up, cousin'.

'Nah, nah, you good', Method A cannot bear to say otherwise.

'A-A. We gonna feast together in the great hall', Method Bee replies.

'We are, you the bravest warlord there ever was', Method A consoles, tears rolling down her wrinkled face.

'You gotta become the one and only warlord. A, kill-kill that Gang-s', Method Bee urges with his last words. He is dead

Method A replies softly, 'Aye'. She holds up a shaka sign in respect. A number of fighters come to help, to alleviate the suffering of the dying. She instructs a couple to lift up her cousin's body and take it to the roof, to reunite him with his wife, Rulez Haah. As per tradition, Jerseyans must be cremated after they die, so that their spirit can transcend to the Chamber of Warriors, they cannot feast in the Great hall otherwise. With so many dead, there will not be the usual elaborate funeral today, just the burning.

They walk together quietly to the roof, where Rulez Haah's dead body still lies. Instructing to lay Method Bee besides,

Method A rips a strip from her purple blouse and walks over to wrapping it across her torn torso. The scene around them is one of utter devastation, many of the hollowed buildings now fully collapsed, the air even more rancid and full of dust. The ground pockmarked with deep holes; Journal is no longer a functioning dwelling.

More Jerseyans have come to the rooftop of the Transportation Center. Many exhausted and badly burnt, their resolve is greater than ever. Method A removes two gold medallions and places one on each chest, taking a moment to reflect in silence. A great many gather with her to mourn and pay their respects, with dead body after dead body laid out.

In memory of Rulez Haah, a 'fair, kind boss', her servants come to sing a Jerseyan song and eulogise her, repeating the same chorus, 'Our mighty warlord, slayer of great evil, rise to the feast. She parties in the great hall forever and ever, our fallen peeps celebrating with her'.

With Houston flying overhead, Pretoria transports down, immediately offering a shaka sign to Method A. Very much shocked by all the destruction, by appearance even worse than that of Queen Elizabeth. The king scorpions, including Ken, brave the hazy light to come outside too. Fortunate to be much more resistant to extreme heat, few have been killed by the red-light of the MLS-Arts ship.

Clenching her fists, Method A's finishes paying her respects to all, remembering Bee's final words 'to become the one and only warlord'. As the servants pour flasks of enoki wine over the bodies and set them alight, Pretoria stands beside Method A. The chorus rises, and the dead bodies burn, their ashes scattering upwards into the acidic clouds. This will go down as one of the darkest days in the history of the Jerseyans.

Pretoria now invites her to join him for discussions. Dr VonHelmann keen to speak to her about officially joining as a member of the EaR. Method A agrees to talk with a nod, thinking of her own aims first - needing support to kill Gangs Hater and fulfil her promise to her cousin to become the one and only warlord.

Before she leaves, she turns to the Jerseyans who have gathered, 'My peeps, pick up your arms, go to Manhattan. We gonna get some revenge! I soon join'. The battle still continues underground with Gangs Hater's Jerseyans at Hoboken station and Exchange Place station.

The Jerseyans throw up a shaka sign, shouting, 'Aye! Revenge, kill Gangs Hater'!

Albeit battle-weary, they all recognise the fight is far from over. Prepared to strike a deal with the EaRA, Method A transports up into Houston's battleship with several of her guards. As the rest of the Jerseyans and king scorpions, including Ken, leave to support the fight in the subway system. Gangs Hater left abandoned, like Colonel Mason, alone to face those he betrayed.

Chapter 12 Schuurman's Lab

VanWest does not let the group rest for long. Eager to press on and find the doctors, Schuurman and King, he leads them back down and over to where the water drained. Hoping to find an exit from the chamber and a path to the Universal Council's hidden base. A voice in his head reassures him that this is the right way.

A thirsty Iris stops briefly to collect some water from a small puddle, before following LeSouris and VanWest into a dim and narrow tunnel. With each step, her emerald ring fades as the cold chill returns. The tunnel reminds VanWest of Stage 2 of the Universal Games, navigating through Pytheas's Labyrinth. Here, he too remains alert for any signs of trouble but this tunnel is not manmade, rather a natural passageway under the Alba Mons mountain range. LeSouris trusts him to lead the way and spends his time rubbing at his fishlike gills in the hope it will somehow go away.

After their successful infiltration of Ward B on the moon base, coming to meet VanWest disguised as Nurse Rose, Iris wants to know if LeSouris can hack the security network of this base too, 'Are you able to hack this Universal base'?

LeSouris nods, 'If same as on moon, rest assured I find the solution'!

Too focused to comment, VanWest does not envision such security on this route. This ancient tunnel predates the Council and its base. Rounding another corner, they stumble upon a strange sight that stops them still, 'Whoa'! Not quite sure what it is and why it is there, they find a spacesuit stuck under some rubble.

It's a design that VanWest has only ever seen in the Enforcer's moon base archives, that belonging to an early third millennia space explorer. The size of an adult male, its helmet sports a dark blue visor and its uniform is white, except for black stripes on its shoulder pads. The spacesuit is very similar to that of an early SpaceX uniform, Earth's first private space exploration company. Curiously, this edition bears no logo, no characteristic X, nor does it have a national flag.

LeSouris kneels down to carefully open its visor, only to jump away, 'Yikes'! Inside is a skeleton. Whoever it was, this explorer was likely caught and trapped by a cave-in. The disappearance of the ice having released him or her from their resting place. This could be good news, a confirmation that this tunnel is, or at least was, connected to the surface; that there is an exit!

Not able to stay and rebury, LeSouris gives a short Utopian prayer, ending with 'may you rest in peace, in Utopia and beyond'.

They must press on. VanWest can sense that they are going in the right direction; the voice in his head growing louder with each step, it keeps calling him - *come*. There is a junction ahead, one leading further down to where the water has drained and the other upwards, on a near-vertical climb. The air above is warmer, unlike in Arcadia Plains, there are no lava flows here, Alba Mons a dormant volcano. Could it be the base?

Colonel Cornelius's coordinates confirm it is close. VanWest signals Iris and LeSouris to follow him up. Already breathing heavily, not quite in his Enforcer shape, they recognise his determination and do not question. As they climb, the path narrows considerably, at its end, there is a piercing light. But, it takes an hour until they reach another junction: one path cutting across, the other continuing vertically.

The light brighter, LeSouris enthusiastically points at symbols and art etched into the jagged, rocky walls around. Most are faded, childlike drawings of flowers and trees, in some places there is still colour - green lines under the sun.

In a jovial voice, LeSouris declares, 'My friends, look more proof of Utopia, yes'? As if having discovered Utopia itself and not just drawings.

'Could be'! Iris replies, taking this moment to take a deep breath. Albeit a Utopian, she is not quite as zealous as LeSouris and her father.

VanWest nods and signals for them to keep going, on the vertical path to where the light originates - the voice still calling. As he proceeds, the passage becomes so narrow that VanWest is forced to crawl. But partway through, he stops still. Like switching from a static to a noisy radio channel, tens of voices call to him at once, *VanWest*!

Overwhelmed, he grabs his head, shaking it wildly. LeSouris and Iris look at each other - a little frightened.

'My love, are you ok'? Iris asks.

He's not. VanWest not only hears multiple voices but can feel their presence: pain and unhappiness. He doesn't answer her and presses on. Even though the path brightens, it also continues to narrow. VanWest, with his broad shoulders, is barely able to fit through and is forced to pull himself up by his elbows.

LeSouris calls over to VanWest, 'My friend, is this the right way'?

Once again, VanWest does not answer. Panting heavily, LeSouris shakes his head and continues to follow. The light comes shining through a small crack ahead, it appears to be the end of the narrow passageway. Worryingly, the gap is only large enough to fit his hand and lower arm through. As he does so, he can feel the warm air circulating in a large space behind. Possibly a ventilation shaft. VanWest realises that this rock's texture is different to the rest, smoother it seems to have been placed here on purpose, perhaps to conceal the passage.

LeSouris and Iris wait, hoping that he can figure a way out. VanWest tries to dislodge the rock with a hard push, but it is firmly stuck in place. Changing tact, he grips the outer edge with his left hand and pulls it inwards. This time it shifts a little. Gathering more strength, he continues to pull, and after several strenuous seconds, the rock finally comes loose. Dislodged, VanWest now pushes it up and out. Falling into the darkness, it strangely does not hit anything, there's no noise at all! The emptiness behind must extend for a mile or more.

LeSouris and Iris are relieved to finally get out this claustrophobic passage. But they are apprehensive at what they might encounter next, deducing by VanWest's manner, not all is well.

'I trust your "love" knows where he's going'? LeSouris whispers to Iris, who answers with a small kick of dirt into his face.

Crawling out, VanWest grips the rocks around to steady himself, such is the steep drop. As suspected, it is a ventilation shaft, designed quite similarly to that on the Universal Council's moon base; the side opposite is cladded with reinforced aluminium sheets. He has found the base!

Following the light, he spots a horizontal shaft above. Gauging the distance to be about 2 meters, VanWest deduces that he should be able to jump across and then pull himself inside. *Jump!* Without notifying the others, he throws himself over the drop, his fingertips just reaching the shaft.

Whoa! A startled Iris calls out, 'VanWest be careful'! Her voice echoing across.

VanWest manages to pull himself up, sliding onto the smooth aluminium panels. The voices rising, he nearly forgets the others until he hears LeSouris whisper.

'Praise be, my friend... Help us next'?

LeSouris offers Iris to go first, advising her to 'not look down'!

VanWest stretches out his arm and hand, 'You ready'?

Another warm breeze passes as Iris grabs hold of his hand, VanWest muscular arms pulling her across and into the shaft. More spacious than the tunnel, its ceiling is still quite low. VanWest does the same for LeSouris, who grimaces as he crosses the pitch-black darkness, again in one motion and without issue.

LeSouris tries once more to ask about the plan, but VanWest moves away too fast, crawling on all fours. Though they know they must proceed, all dread what they might encounter. For VanWest, the painful feelings grow even more intense. A vision returns, the semi-naked man in a medical bib, this time he is looks at him straight in the eyes, he mouths *come*.

Not knowing what happened in New Jersey and the Enforcers joining the EaRA to counter Commissioner Ming, they can only remain hopeful and focus on fulfilling their part. They are so close. A low buzzing noise rises as they continue crawling towards the light's source, which they soon locate comes through a mesh net, a brightly lit room below.

Tall shelves pack the room, the closet filled with beakers and petri dishes. They realise that the buzzing comes from an alarm, a red light is flashing. It's Schuurman's lab all right, and it's on high alert! VanWest wonders what this means, have they been discovered? Or, is this a general level of alert, with the Space Army preparing to go to Earth?

VanWest whispers to Iris and LeSouris, 'I must go inside. Let me check the room is clear of hostiles first'.

LeSouris nods, 'Good idea'.

Iris responds in a low voice, 'No, we are going together'!

'Ok... We send update to your father first. Yes'? LeSouris answers.

Iris agrees. It upsets her slightly, a reminder that there have been no messages from the EaRA since landing in Arcadia Plains, she hopes this not to be a bad sign. But chooses to keep her worries to herself, VanWest looks burdened enough.

VanWest takes out his Quantum Communicator, entering Dr VonHelmann's code *01034589X*, noting their current situation and confirming that the *Base Is Found. Space Army On Alert. Pilot Of Method A - Gs Dead. Dr King Not Yet Located.* Opting though to not mention the icy chamber and mural, unable to explain.

The voices in his head grow louder, excited by his approach - *come*, they call. He looks to lift open the mesh barrier, not realising that his hands are shaking. None of them are armed, having only just escaped from Arcadia Plains with their lives. The choice is stark, the pressure is on them to fulfil their part in this 'New Beginning'.

'My friend, you tell us finally your plan'? He adds half-jokingly, 'I worry my charm not enough to disarm Space Soldier'!

VanWest still cannot articulate his plan, he feels that these voices are key to their success and that all will be revealed inside. He replies, reminding him of his faith, 'You trust'?

LeSouris sighs before nodding, 'I trust, of course'.

A skilled infiltrator, LeSouris offers to help remove the mesh, 'Let me'. He gently taps the screws with his long fingernails, slowly loosening them as he does so, and then lifts the mesh up, quietly placing it to one side, 'My friend, easy'! Having come from under the mountain, they have thus far evaded the security network, VanWest now enters the lab. He hangs from the vent and swings his legs to the top of the nearest metal shelf, the highest point in the room, careful to not knock any beakers.

Skilfully, he makes it across - the beakers only clattering slightly. He next helps LeSouris and Iris over, as quietly and carefully as possible and they climb down the shelf to the floor. This place stores a whole range of laboratory items: syringes, glass jars and boxes of latex gloves. However, there too are items that seem out of place, in fact, some altogether bizarre and not quite of this world.

On one shelf, VanWest is surprised to find the blue and green featured headdress he saw when the ghost of the little girl touched his hand, there too is a dagger made of flint with a wooden handle, snakelike symbols intricately carved into it. These very same items he saw on Dr Schuurman. It must be a sign that whatever is fated draws closer.

Further, in the centre of the room and partly concealed under a white plastic cover is a large disc shape stone. It's the stone sermon! Repeatedly carved all around with a mysterious face: rounds eyes, fangs and a crown. Removing the cover, VanWest finds more intricate designs. Its symbols near undecipherable, he assumes it to be a calendar of sorts.

As VanWest touches it, there's a new vision. Dr Schuurman's holds a still-beating heart in the palm of his hand, his eyes stare straight at his eyes, menaced and crazed, as if right in front of him. His snarly teeth and face now too covered in its blood. A lone voice breaks him from his vision - *come*. It directs him to a small door at the end of the room, controlling his mind it forces VanWest to walk towards it.

Crash! The shattering of glass jolts him back. He turns to find LeSouris gasping, having half-fainted and fallen backwards onto the white stone floor - his saggy fishlike gills covering his face.

Iris comes to his aid. Crouching down, she asks him, 'Are you ok'?

Shaking his head, he looks up at VanWest with horror in his eyes as if he were something strange and inhuman. Bending down to pick up the broken petri dish, VanWest finally understands, the voices, the Colonel's last words of 'beware yourself', and the victory parade after the Universal Games. All the petri dishes on this shelf are labelled with the prefix *V-A-N-W-E-S-T*.

Iris is quick to understand, embracing him she whispers, 'VanWest, I'm sorry'.

She had suspected something awful like this, remembering too the parade after the Universal Games, where a lookalike of VanWest stood beside Dr King, while he lay in Ward B linked up to a Schuurman Reporting Monitor (SRM). Iris shakes her head, she wonders what else her father has kept from her. This is not the only revelation on this trip, her father having never discussed her emerald ring, its origins.

'My word, my word, I cannot believe it'! LeSouris mutters, a tinge of colour returning to his cheeks.

Looking at Iris and LeSouris, VanWest reveals yet another chilling detail, 'I hear them'!

'What'? Iris says.

'Please, not scare me more'! LeSouris replies.

VanWest doesn't just hear the voices, he feels them, their pain so very intense. Iris holds him tightly as more dark images flash through his mind. Like a bad forgotten memory suddenly recalled, he relives his beginning, watching as a ginger-haired Dr Schuurman stand beside a nurse who surveys a line of incubators, each labelled *Van der Westhuizen*, followed by a number. Schuurman suddenly stops in front of one, labelled *A1*, and grabs hold of the nurse's arm. He smiles widely at the sound of crying coming from within.

'Nurse Rose, send for Dr VonHelmann. Tell him one survived'!

Panning out, he can see more incubators, many of which contain babies that don't look quite normal; many horribly deformed. Only one looks healthy, *A1*, a crying baby boy. Schuurman looks joyfully down and prods him with his finger, laughing loudly as he does. His pleasure so intense at hearing him cry, 'At last'!

The scene suddenly returns to that of Dr Schuurman standing menacingly over the large stone. Wearing his blue and green featured headdress, his dagger dropping down on his naked body. VanWest reopens his eyes.

Having pinched his arm, Iris asks, 'What are you doing'?

VanWest doesn't quite know, muttering disconnected words, 'Going somewhere... somewhere beyond horror, this place... place of my creation, birthplace... inexplicable evil'.

Iris embraces him tightly again, 'I am here for you... We will make it together'. And shakes him gently, 'You are not a number. You are VanWest. You are my love'!

A solemn tear rolls down VanWest's cheek as he speaks of his creation, 'I'm an experiment, a clone of a Martian, one of the poor souls that were murdered. His name President Van der Westhuizen. I've seen his face, that too of his daughter'.

'Oh, my love'.

What VanWest hadn't known was that he was one of many such clones, 'So much suffering'. He relives and feels their 'painful, terrible deaths'.

Iris places her soft hands on his cheeks, wiping away his lone tear, 'VanWest, you are you! Shaped by your own experiences. You are the boy I kissed under the stairs, the boy I fell in love with, the man that rescued me, that started the insurrection. You are no longer alone. We'll make sure no one else suffers'.

VanWest kisses her on the forehead. He wonders what her father did here when Head of Science, he remembers that the cloning of Van der Westhuizen was deemed unsuccessful, could this be due to his sabotage. One voice, louder than the rest, breaks him from his thoughts, again urging him to go through the tiny door.

'VanWest... tell me what is behind that door'? LeSouris asks him, having recomposed himself and gotten back to his feet.

But VanWest instead tells him to 'turn back'. He repeats, 'Turn back, take my sweet Iris with you'.

Iris is having none of it, grabbing a discarded metal table leg, 'We've come this far, no way am I leaving you now. My father, Pretoria, the citizens are not just relying on you'.

LeSouris picks up a metal bar too, 'They rely on all of us'. Offering an ejaculatory prayer, 'Today is fated. Let us trust in Utopia. Let it protect us'.

VanWest looks at Iris, with her approval he places his hand against the door. *Screech!* It slowly opens, its noise reminding him of his chalk breaking against his, now dead, professor's blackboard, Master Jiang. Revealing a dimly lit corridor. He closes his eyes briefly and steps inside, LeSouris and Iris following, ready with their makeshift weapons. The stench here is most foul, that of rotten flesh.

On the right side, VanWest finds many discarded cribs stacked up, they too bearing his name, *V-A-N-W-E-S-T*. These are not directly clones of Van der Westhuizen, rather of him. On the left side are more metal shelves, packed with glass jars. A sharp pain shoots through his head as he looks closer, each contains a tiny organ, a human heart!

He looks across, row upon row of hearts are suspended, floating in a liquid medium. For Iris, the sight and smell is too much to bear, she begins to gag. Yet there are more disturbing items, including a shelf full of tiny skulls, strangely painted blue and decorated with jade stones. It all makes for a most cruel collection - that of his dead clones.

If it were not clear already, he, not Van der Westhuizen, is the forbearer to this latest large-scale cloning operation; he is the clone source. Those deemed unsuccessful, their bodies have been dissected and parts removed. VanWest cannot bear to see more but the voices, those he now figures are his clones, keep calling him onwards to the corridor's end. Adrenaline coursing through their bodies, LeSouris and Iris continue shoulder-to-shoulder, assuming a defensive triangle. VanWest stops before the door, the voices reaching a crescendo. They all know they must proceed, their fate and that of Earth dependent on killing Dr King. He has foreseen the Interrogator, who resides on Dr King's SCC-400, is in the lab. He knows he is close - a link to the doctor.

VanWest places his hand against the door as he tells the others to 'get ready'.

As it opens, a dim blue light breaks through, followed by agonising cries that shudder down their spines. They go forward and find themselves in a large cathedral ceiling chamber, which must reach 20 feet high. As far as the eye can see, there are lines of incubators, deformed and decayed bodies lying in many. A sight so awful that Iris momentarily hides behind VanWest's shoulder. This place that he foresaw in his visions, its grimy decor and incubators, smells even more rancid - a mix of decomposing flesh and antiseptic.

Blue neon lights overhang a number of cribs, a remarkably odd choice as blue light makes babies hyper - likely another of Dr Schuurman's experiments. A red cross marks each, with a number prefixed by *V-A-N-W-E-S-T*. Their tiny, dead bodies entangled in a web of metallic tubes. VanWest walks further inside,

LeSouris and Iris keeping their metal bar's aloft, the voices call him over to the other side of this huge, dimly lit room.

Iris and LeSouris faces turn even paler, doing well to not convulse as each footstep, however faint, echoes across. Whoever is here must have heard their approach by now, yet no one comes to meet them. LeSouris starts to speak lowly to himself, reciting Utopian prayers to give them courage, as well as to bless the dead babies in the cribs.

As they walk further, he finds from where the cries originate, from several living and breathing babies in a row of incubators. Their eyes and skin painfully inserted with tubes and wires. VanWest hurries to them, his heartaches, their pain so intense. Each is oblivious to where and who they are; innocent and lost. As LeSouris and Iris join VanWest, the babies' heads shift all at once. 'Whoa'! LeSouris jumps back. Their eyes are not of VanWest's, not grey; they are instead red and beady, just like that of the Space Soldiers. It is worse than VanWest thought: these babies, not wholly his clones after all, rather a genetically engineered Martian and cyborg mix.

'Welcome home'!

VanWest turns to find his lookalike with the medical bib staring at him. Albeit slightly shorter and thinner, the man is a near-exact copy, his face, his eyes the same. This one is not his clone, rather like him that of President Van der Westhuizen. It is the little boy that he remembers playing with as a child, the man standing next to Dr King during the Universal Games' victory parade. Indeed, his identical twin brother.

LeSouris and Iris are left completely bewildered, unsure if to swing their makeshift weapons at this lookalike or not. They look for a cue from VanWest, THEIR VanWest.

His twin keeps smiling, almost stupidly, before offering his hand, repeating once more, 'Welcome home'.

VanWest doesn't know how to react, too stunned to speak. He has always felt a presence, perhaps all through his life, but on Mars he has finally found from where it originates. But something is not quite right with this twin; physically, they are similar, mentally they are not.

Before he can shake his clone twin's hand, a ginger-haired man steps out from the shadows. A man he has come to see more and more often in his visions, Dr Minus Schuurman. His grin unbearably wide, his lab coat stained from blood and sweat. This man exudes only evil.

Dr Schuurman greets him, 'Van der Westhuizen A-one! Welcome back home'!

Chapter 13 VanWest

Iris instinctively steps forward to confront Dr Schuurman, only for VanWest to pull her back - it's not safe.

Casting his eyes over those lying in all the cribs, VanWest asks him, 'Why'?

Dr Schuurman continues to grin widely, 'Welcome home'!

VanWest asks again more forcefully, 'Tell me, WHY'?

'Patience, A-one! Let us first reacquaint ourselves. We have been expecting you, ever since New Jersey'. And then oddly starts to giggle, 'What an effort to smuggle yourself to come to meet us. You could have just called'!

VanWest isn't surprised. It all makes sense, Dr Schuurman indeed knew he was coming; the state of high alert in the lab, the Inspector in the port, even the ability to reach Mars by itself unlikely given the clampdown on the Jerseyan cargo ships.

'I asked you, why'? VanWest still demands an answer - even though he already knows what it is.

Dr Schuurman still giggling, 'Ah, you are an impatient one, well... not really one... Let me introduce thou twin brother - A-one-zero-three. You both the surviving Van der Westhuizen clones. So hard to recreate, you two not quite human are you... rather you are Martian'.

'This is not what I asked'!

Dr Schuurman finally answers, 'Behold, for thou clones are the future. Picture Space Soldiers enhanced with your abilities, a world where deviants are caught before even committing a crime. The Universal all-knowing, all-powerful... You deserve some congratulations... Afterall A-one, your DNA is part of it all now'.

Not only are they cloning VanWest for his psychic traits they too enhance with cybernetics, creating a new breed of Universal Space Soldier. This, the next level. Dr Schuurman points ominously at the babies, 'Before the Universal Games, we thought your abilities, your psychic senses were not tameable. But you proved it was worth retrying'!

VanWest shakes his head, he can't bear to hear that their torture, the jars of hearts, the painted skulls, is all because he won the Universal Games. His ability having been rediscovered after he was injured and his mind read by the SRM.

VanWest's clone twin, Van der Westhuizen A103, offers his hand once more and repeats, 'Welcome home'!

His twin has the same grey eyes, but are glazed over and empty. VanWest looks to Dr Schuurman, 'What's is wrong with him'?

'Oh dear, A1, you have noticed... Experiments can have different outcomes, some better than others', Dr Schuurman replies coldly.

Iris pushes VanWest's hand away and steps forward, her face now bright red with anger, 'You sick piece of roach'!

VanWest's twin A103 reacts to what he perceives to be an incoming attack and in one motion removes her metal bar, disarming and shoving her to the floor. Incensed to see Iris harmed, VanWest rushes at him, LeSouris in tow, striking him with a hard punch to the side of his head. LeSouris following with a strike of his metal bar to his shoulder. A103 falls backwards, less well-built having spent the majority of his existence inside this lab, he is no match for his Enforcer twin.

Instead of being alarmed or annoyed, Dr Schuurman starts clapping, 'Very good, very good'! Very much enjoying the fight.

BAD VANWEST! Many voices call to him at once, upset with him striking A103. He looks into the shadows, from out of the darkness along the laboratory's walls figures emerge into the dim blue light. He finds not 1, not 4, but 11 younger versions staring at him. All with red eyes, their jumpsuits labelled *VANWEST BV73*, these his newer, cyborg versions.

Dr Schuurman's snarly teeth showing, 'Congratulations are in order. May I introduce thou to well you... a rather sumptuous bunch, thou children'!

VanWest is left aghast, not only are these a cyborg mix of him but Dr Schuurman has sped up their ageing process. Their proportions that of him at thirteen years old, their arms though that of a muscular man with biceps even bigger than his own. They crowd together and move forward as one, ready to pounce as Dr Schuurman steps behind, watching with glee.

LeSouris helps Iris from the concrete floor and gestures to VanWest to move back, towards the blackened glass on an adjacent wall. Where he spots a well-camouflaged door at its centre, thinking it to be a possible exit.

VanWest doesn't want to fight his clones, despite their size, he can sense they are mentally the age of toddlers. They do not fully understand what is happening, scared to disobey Dr Schuurman, they also want to know more about VanWest, their clone source A1. Unbeknownst to Dr Schuurman, they see VanWest as a sort of father figure. They, like him, also feel pain for the dead and suffering babies. They too understand at some level that this lab is evil.

As the trio retreats backwards, the door behind slides open, sending a stream of bright light into the room. From within, two figures emerge, neither though is their target Dr King, they are however two men VanWest has come to know all too well. First the snake-like Interrogator, still wearing his amber stone pendant, and the second Commissioner Ming in his black peaked cap. Having recently arrived from Earth, the Commissioner has finally caught up with his *Most Wanted*. The blackened glass concealing an observation room, from where they have been watching this whole time.

The dangling of the pendant triggers a thought, its amber stone looks remarkably similar to that the little girl was holding outside the church, in his vision during the trip to Mars. VanWest wonders if this is the other missing piece from the mural. If brighter, it would match.

Dr Schuurman, Commissioner Ming and the Interrogator all snigger, amused to watch VanWest's clones slowly surround the trio. Now concussed, A103 picks himself from the floor and cowers behind.

The Commissioner speaks first, in his usual condescending tone, 'VanWest, or should I say A-one, so good of you to grace us with your presence. I see you have met your twin brother and clones'.

Turning to Dr Schuurman, he congratulates him on his cloning operation, admiring the BV73s, 'You have excelled yourself. I see the oldest batch of Space Soldiers is close to ready for our return to Earth'.

VanWest grimaces at the thought of them using his DNA, Martian DNA to commit the genocide of the Earth's citizens.

'Dear Commissioner, they are so. Unlike VanWest, thou can rest assured that his clones are much better. Their Martian weaknesses, namely naivety, are expunged and their ability enhanced'.

VanWest's attention stays on the Interrogator. Who licks his lips as he continues to dangle the pendant provocatively, just like when torturing him on the SCC-400. If he is here, then Dr King must be close by. Maybe even behind the one-way blackened glass, in the observation room - yet he does not reveal himself.

Much angered by all that has happened on Earth, the Commissioner hectors VanWest, 'Be sure, your Martian species were weak. So very naïve, inferior. I am glad Schuurman fixes your clones. Free of this Martian gullibility, they have only your one strength, your one ability'. Referring to his psychic sense.

The Commissioner then points at Iris, 'Her father, the Utopian deviant Mad Newton, tried to keep your ability from us. He can be sure now that the Universal is all-knowing, all-powerful. He has failed'.

The Interrogator praises, 'Salve, salve THE U-NI-VER-SSS-ALLL'!

The blackened glass lights up and then fades. Revealing Gs bloodied and bruised face pressed against it, his eyes gouged out. He is dead. Iris and LeSouris wince at the sight, but for the Interrogator and Dr Schuurman, it prompts yet more nefarious giggling. Iris steps on her makeshift weapon, the metal table leg, and picks it up. VanWest's twin A103 continues to watch from behind his master as the BV73 clones step closer. He tells VanWest - *sorry*.

The Commissioner rubs his hands, excited to see them attack their Enforcer forebear. But VanWest still believes his clones can be reasoned with, he addresses them mind-to-mind and joins in their chatter, keeping his message simple to understand, *Schuurman bad man, murderer*.

VanWest repeats the words, *bad man*.

Although this meeting was fated, his coming to Mars and the lab, VanWest has learnt the future is not one-dimensional. Like on Judgement Day, when he stopped the execution of Iris by Captain Alpha coming true. Others such as the explosion in the UNESCO conference in 1951 Paris and the ISS shuttle in 1998 Florida never coming to pass. He knows his clones can see this too; having seen his coming and all that has, will happen. Even if they do not fully understand.

VanWest tells them to *change our future*.

Not yet instructing to kill, Schuurman wants to scold Iris's father further, his predecessor and former Head of Science. Walking between his clones and up to Iris, his putrid breath wafting in her face.

'That liar, that deviant your father! Mad Newton kept A-one's ability a secret. His cloning a success. He tricked me, bringing with it embarrassment. He should have known that no one can stop progress'. But the wide grin returns, somewhat cryptically in a lower voice he tells her, 'Oh well, he gives me a wonderful gift now. I will use it well to bring a glorious new past, present and future'.

VanWest is too busy trying to communicate with his clone children to notice and understand his words. Mind-to-mind, he repeats to them the same simple message, *bad man*, highlighting next the suffering in the lab, *so much pain*. It's not clear if Dr Schuurman knows he can communicate with them without speaking, but the words are having an effect, their chatter intensifies as they question their master - *bad man*.

Unintimidated, Iris shouts at the Commissioner and Dr Schuurman, 'The Council's greed knows no end, never satisfied, always wanting more, with no care to whoever gets hurt. You say VanWest is gullible, why? Because he dares to speak the truth'!

The Commissioner sneers, 'Oh, you fool. It's so... well, Van der Westhuizen of you! So gullible to not see this mad deviant your father is manipulating you, just as he did Van der Westhuizen. You think he loves you... Dear poor Iris, he only cares for himself'.

'You lie'! Iris objects.

Recalling what happened on Mars, 'Let me tell you a tale...'

Once upon a time,
the Council found a planet,
there lived a mutant race
that worshipped a green light.
So naïve and trusting,
they made the perfect prey.

What nerve they had,
they thought they could teach
the Council to follow their way.

With a treaty signed,
they gave their key to a diplomat.
Inviting us in with open arms.
The Universal Council then made...

The Martians no more.

This 'tale' reminds VanWest of *Our* Stone. This the key that unlocked *Our Energy*, which had protected the Martians. The energy depicted in the child-like drawings with the green lines. It finally clicks; could it be the little girl with the stone, the large slab in the church, the mural, are all be connected to Mars's defences becoming undone?

Glancing at Iris's emerald ring and then the amber stone the Interrogator holds, not wholly valuable these items do not warrant being kept so closely for centuries, he must have known its significance - this the 'interplanetary diplomat' of which the Commissioner speaks. Adding yet more urgency, he MUST retrieve the pendant from the Interrogator.

LeSouris challenges, mocking him, 'May I continue the tale for you...'

This Council most wicked,
had a weakness too,
call it great hubris or great arrogance.
They thought their roach goo smell of roses...

But praise be to Utopia!
Like the best of stories,
this too has happy ending...

Utopia rose again and this wickedness,
you all,
disappear!

With his clones squabbling amongst themselves, VanWest makes his move, he rounds one of the clones and strikes at Dr Schuurman, hitting him square in the upper chest and sending him flying back into the arms of VanWest's cowering twin, A103.

'Attack, attack'! Dr Schuurman commands all.

They do not obey. Instead, one of the BV73 clones turns and puts Dr Schuurman in a chokehold, tossing A103 out of the way as if a ragdoll. Remembering Colonel Cornelius's last words to kill both doctors, VanWest urges him on - *kill bad man. Agh!* The clone drags him into the shadows as the doctor screams, 'Help, help me'!

Shocked, the Interrogator and Commissioner step back. Never having thought the clones could turn on them; sure that they were all firmly under the doctor's control.

Screech! A high-pitched sound stuns all, a safety mechanism activated, but the clones are undeterred. They charge at the Interrogator and Commissioner, who just about manage to race back into the observation room and lock the door behind. VanWest wills the clones to attack the locked door, repeating his simple message, *bad man.* The combined strength of the clones is so strong that within seconds the reinforced door and glass surround is broken. Storming through, the BV73 clones give chase as VanWest, alongside Iris and LeSouris, do their best to keep up.

Several patrol androids jolt out from the wall to block the clones' path, but the BV73s cannot be stopped, they swarm, ducking and then jumping together to dodge several volleys of shots. They think and work together as one, the clones at the front sliding underneath and breaking their metallic legs, the others then snapping their long metal arms off as if they were matchsticks.

As the BV73s charge into the next corridor, VanWest hears new voices calling to him. He looks right to find not cribs but rather locked rooms with small windows. On the reinforced prison-like doors is a metal nameplate, *V-A-N-W-E-S-T.*

Through the window, he can see yet more of his clones, albeit smaller than the BV73s, the metal plates hold a new prefix *BZ.* Their eyes beady and red. His clones plead to go free and join the others. Iris and LeSouris catch up and are equally shocked by what they encounter. VanWest moves them out of the way as one of the BV73 clones returns to break the door down, charging the door he soon breaks it open. The children, in turn, follow out and break open the other reinforced doors all along the corridor.

The clone swarm grows, joining together with the other BV73s that fast approach a fleeing Interrogator, now trailing the Commissioner by a few yards. VanWest struggles to hear his own thoughts, his mind overloaded by all the voices. The number of clones reaches 100 strong, whilst varying in size, each is muscular, strong and fast. All are also mute, having never had the need to develop their vocal muscles.

Waaahhhh! Before the clones can seize the Interrogator, a siren blares. And red-eyed Universal Space Soldiers surge from the transportation room. The Interrogator immediately points his index finger at the clones, instructing to engage, 'Sss-HOOT'!

However, the Space Soldiers do not. The clones stop still and huddle together, chatting amongst themselves, unsure how to proceed. Born to be Space Soldiers, they too recognise these cyborgs as somewhat kindred, lab creations. VanWest implores them to attack, desperate to get the pendant and amber stone back. Only for a stalemate of sorts to ensue. Connecting mind-to-mind, he repeats to them the same simple message - *bad man.*

As VanWest urges them on, a high-ranking Space Soldier emerges, one VanWest recognises immediately as the Universal Games red team leader, Lt. Colonel Omega. His face badly scarred, still wearing his thick and bright red shoulder pads. Sensing VanWest's concern, the clones fall silent, from cybernetic, hardy fighters they become frightened children once more. Some even look ready to turn and run back to their cells.

Lt. Colonel Omega commands them to do so, 'Return. Repeat Return. Do NOT defy'!

VanWest knows he must remove his own doubts and show courage. He MUST set an example for all to follow. Stepping forward, he walks through his clones to face them. The Space Soldiers present their Plasma blasters, threatening to shoot. Sensing his bravery, one of the BV73 clones responds by joining him, stepping forward to stand shoulder-to-shoulder with him. Their posturing and courage rally the others, who all step forward together as one. Lt. Colonel Omega losing his opportunity to capitalise on their indecision.

VanWest wonders why the Space Soldiers do not shoot. His first thought that it could be due to the risk of causing a cave-in.

This base not a slick and ultra-modern structure like that on the moon, rather a throwback and relic of a bygone age when the Council took over Mars. He thinks further, with Dr Schuurman gone there is no one close to authorise this engagement. He realises that the Lt. Colonel is not ranked high enough to kill these clones. It must be a doctor.

'Cease, desist, return to your rooms'! Lt. Colonel Omega repeats. With no response, he barks even louder, 'OBEY ME'!

VanWest barks back, 'That's NOT going to happen'!

The Lt. Colonel bluffs, 'The Space Soldiers will commence firing... RETURN'.

Much to the disconcertment of Iris and LeSouris, unaware of what is happening, the clones react by taking another step forward.

VanWest bravely challenges the Lt. Colonel Omega individually, 'Come fight me! One-on-one... Pick on someone your own size, you pathetic minion of Dr King'.

The clones are even more encouraged by him, looking at him with hero-like awe. For once this cyborg, Lt. Colonel Omega, looks more human than machine. Still, with no authorisation to engage, he edges backwards to the transporter. A sign of weakness that triggers the clones into action as they charge in unison - VanWest joining, with Iris and LeSouris in tow.

Lt. Colonel Omega flees into the transporter, knocking the Interrogator out of his way. His Space Soldiers left helpless, unsure of how to engage. VanWest muscles past, his focus still very much on catching the wretched Interrogator. Just about reaching him as he enters the transporter, tackling him to the floor.

But, as he rips the pendant from around the Interrogator's neck, the transporter lights up and, in a flash, he finds himself out of Schuurman's lab and the secret base. Lying on his back with the amber stone in his hand, the Interrogator a short distance away. They have arrived alone, all around them a vast expanse of red sand and rock that stretches as far as the eye can see.

Chapter 14 One Warlord

Dr VonHelmann and Captain Kun-lee appear via the communicator, standing in 4D beside Pretoria. With Method having had time to replenish with some food and drink, Dr VonHelmann requests a discussion on joining the EaRA and this 'New Beginning'. Despite the need for their support, Method A is wary to talk with the Utopian leader. Only knowing him as Mad Newton; a crazed scientist 'hell-bent' on taking Earth backwards. Further, she is suspicious of Utopianism, LeSouris hiding his *U tattoo* every time they meet. A religion and ideology that she fears threatens her own culture and customs.

'Welcome, Method A'! Dr VonHelmann is first to speak.

She looks at Pretoria, asking in a derisory voice, 'You trust him, aye'?

Trying to engage in cordial dialogue, Dr VonHelmann continues, 'Method A, I am so pleased that we finally meet. Thy such a great warrior and warlord. With our rescue of New Jersey, this New Beginning becomes thy too'.

'Your rescue'?

Pretoria's relationship with Method A long-standing, he tries to mediate, 'We make together Earth's Resistance. Free Enforcer, Rebel, Utopian, VanWest against common enemy. You make... Join'?

'VanWest! Many peeps die, all start with him, aye'?

Pretoria defends, 'No... fault of Council'!

Captain Kun-lee defends more staunchly, knowing VanWest well, having been squad members, 'This all started with Dr King, the Elites and the Council. This destruction is their destruction, not

VanWest's. PATH or no PATH, you were always at risk, your casino escapes, your Papini crop all that protected you. Like us, the Free Enforcers, you can now seize this chance to become truly free'!

Method A tries to wrap her mind around this new alliance. She knows she has to cut a deal in order to become the one and only warlord of the Jerseyans. 'Chill dawg... I think it cute, you free, work with NEA. Little strange, aye'?

'Indeed'! Captain Kun-lee half-smiles back.

'Make strange', Pretoria laughs, looking over at Kun-lee. Exchanging a light-hearted moment that seems to soothe the mood.

Dr VonHelmann watches in a calculating manner. He stays connected to VanWest via the Quantum Communicator and feels emboldened after news of the Council's base being found. Yet, he chooses to keep this information to himself as well as the news of Gs's death, seeing that it could prove useful emotional leverage, another one of her closest 'peeps' dead. Likewise, he also chooses not to update VanWest and his daughter, wanting to keep the pressure on them to succeed - fearing news of his EaRA's growth may make the trio complacent.

Method A's tone friendlier, 'I'm a fair A, we find deal'.

'You have the floor', Dr VonHelmann encourages.

She lays out the conditions for her involvement with the EaRA that they must first help her dispose of her rival, 'Gangs Hater, Warlord of New York, sided with the Universal. We kill, his territory, ships mine... ships I lend, you get me? Aye'?

Method A's knows she doesn't hold the strongest hand at this negotiating table, most of her cargo ships have been either destroyed or impounded by the Universal Council. But she's a hard-nosed negotiator, a big part of her success in becoming a warlord. Her offer is compelling, Gangs Hater's cargo ships have remained untouched, up-armoured they could make very good defensive ships to counter the Universal Council's spaceships. They are also well-suited for long-distance space travel.

Pretoria and Kun-lee understand and exchange a nod; they like her deal to help dispose of Gangs Hater in exchange for his ships. Much like Colonel Mason, the Universal Council has abandoned this warlord, in what appears to be a deliberate move by the Commissioner. Mason's Enforcers were used to weaken the Free Enforcers, NEA rebels. By having attacked the Jerseyans next, they allow the Space Army an easier return to exert full control over Earth. The EaRA need Gangs Hater's cargo ships!

'Make good', Pretoria replies.

'Affirmative', Captain Kun-lee replies next.

Dr VonHelmann is pleased to have more ships. With a lone MLS-Arts ship able to cause so much damage without even entering Earth's orbit he knows he must meet them over Mars. There too is some concern for his daughter, but winning is his ultimate objective. But he does not think the deal goes far enough. His aspirations are greater.

Dr VonHelmann pushes back, 'Method A if we accept thy condition, we need you to officially join in Earth's Resistance. You, an official member of this alliance, announcing to all thy Jerseyans that you are EaR'.

Suspicious of his motives, Method A replies angrily, 'Nah-nah, not good. I see why they call you Mad Newton'! Prompting sniggering from her guards.

Even in a best-case scenario, with Dr King killed and the Universal Council's leadership structure undone, Dr VonHelmann knows it will need replacing to maintain order on Earth. He wants the EaR to control this New Beginning, to replace the Universal Council everywhere throughout the Solar System. The Jerseyans fully under his control and eventually followers of Utopianism.

Dr VonHelmann now decides to use the news he held back as leverage, 'Great warlord Method A... Dr King and the Universal Council kill thy Jerseyans, thy cousin. I must tell thee too thy pilot Gs. My sincere condolences'.

Method A reacts in disbelief, 'Nah! You lie'!

Pretoria confirms, 'Me make sorry'.

Method A punches the wall, 'Gs, good bruva'.

Embellishing the success of the resistance, Dr VonHelmann continues, 'VanWest closes in on Dr King on Mars. Join us if you seek real vengeance, not just against this traitor Gangs Hater, the doctor's puppet. Once VanWest succeeds, we will be the partners you seek'. Adding a veiled threat, 'Think of a prosperous future for thy Jerseyans. Our trade and economics will be needed. This can all come true if part of the EaR'.

A clever if not cruel move, Dr VonHelmann knows that Method A needs the lucrative Papini trade to maintain power. Highlighting that with Dr King and the Elites gone, the traditional trade routes will be over, Method A risks not having the riches and resources to hold this expanded territory without his support.

Captain Kun-lee offers his condolences next, 'Method A, sorry for your losses. The Free Enforcers suffer too, your enemy is our enemy. Whatever you decide, you have our support to depose of this warlord, Gangs Hater'. Drawing an annoyed look from Dr VonHelmann, having wanted him to pressurise her further.

Captain Kun-lee instead calms Method A once again. Her thirst for vengeance is stronger than ever but agreeing to formally join in the EaRA is too big a step, at least for now. Nevertheless, her support marks a significant moment; Jerseyans, NEA rebels, Utopians and, now free, Enforcers working together against the Universal Council. This, unfathomable only a little while ago.

Walking over to the holomap, Method A reveals her cunning plan to get to Gangs Hater, whilst avoiding any more ships being destroyed, 'Talk about joining Earth Resist later. In Manhattan, my contact Keys will help me kill Gangs, she gonna get me around security'.

She runs through her plan, drawing it out on the map:

- *Gangs located close to World Trade Center station*
- *Land at Christopher Street station 1 mile away*
- *Take 25 minutes fast walk down Hudson Street to Chambers Street*
- *Located here, Keys cargo bay route underground*

- *She takes us here, to Gangs last known position*

Method A only needs the support of the EaRA to create a diversion; to keep Gangs Hater and his cannons focused away from her on the ground. Pointing at Houston and Captain Kun-lee, 'Battleships fly in the air, keep Gangs ships distracted. Me, Pretoria, my guards enter PATH from ground via Keys's Cargo Bay. Aye'?

Pretoria agrees, 'Make good'.

Her contact Keys is a manager of a cargo bay situated deep inside Gangs Hater's territory, she holds an unguarded entryway into the PATH network, a path to where intelligence indicates Gangs Hater coordinates his defence.

Dr VonHelmann is impressed, deciding to wait till afterwards to continue pressing on her joining the EaR officially. He approves, 'Very good'.

Method A adds, 'Destroy no Gangs's ship, you dawgz want them, you not blow them up'!

'You got it, warlord'! Houston replies, 'We'll do our best to keep them Gangs boys and girls distracted'.

Method A throws up a shaka sign, communicating to all her remaining cargo ships to join the fleet of the EaRA, their combined number 570 strong. If she is made warlord of all, she will have New York's cargo ships to lend, up to 250 more ships - if none are destroyed or damaged.

Her pilot signalling her, 'You ready, boss'? One of only a few of Method A's pilots to have survived unharmed after the attack by the Commissioner and the spaceships.

Due to Gangs Hater's decision to betray, New York has been left untouched. And Method A wants it to remain this way, an area of high Papini production and commercial activity, it will be a lucrative capture needed for rebuilding.

'Sista, ready'! Method A goes to the transporter, and Sista Pee beams her over. Pretoria follows next, taking a protective hazmat mask and a small laser NEA blaster, known as the Plasma Destroyer. A good choice, designed for skirmishes in the sewage tunnels of the Antarctic settlements, not too dissimilar to the tunnels of PATH.

'Keep yourself safe, big guy'! Houston bids farewell.

Pretoria replies, 'Make safe too'.

Houston takes command of Method A's other cargo ships, instructing them to enter a defensive formation with her battleships, with a focus on 'high manoeuvrability and strong shields'.

Whilst the shields of the patrolships are not the best, Captain Kun-lee opts to focus on their strength, their nimbleness. He informs, 'Houston, my ships will fly ahead to draw fire'.

Keen to stay out of harm's way, Dr VonHelmann opts to hang back on the SCC-40 piloted by Lt. Colonel Wang. The motley fleet then proceeds with haste to Manhattan to commence the plan and create the diversion. They must move fast if her plan is to work - little to no ships being damaged.

Boom! Soon reaching Manhattan, Gangs Hater's cannons immediately fire. Captain Kun-lee instructs the patrolships to only intercept incoming shots, hoping this feint attack strategy will work. Like in Journal Square, the Jerseyans are ill-prepared to counter incursions from the air, each of their shots easily neutralised. Gangs Hater's ships also counter, these harder to avoid. They too are up-armoured and engage the EaRA and Method A's cargo ships.

As per the plan, Method A transports onto the surface level about one mile away from Key's cargo bay, alongside Pretoria and her five Jerseyan guards. Avoiding the PATH network, they proceed on foot through the toxic air walking southwards along a rubble-strewn road, Hudson Street. The ruins of Manhattan's skyscrapers are much higher than any in New Jersey. Albeit hollowed-out concrete shells, many still reach over 40 stories high and provide some welcome shade. Having once held 10 times the population in this relatively small area, it holds many more underground networks than New Jersey, supporting a large populace of around one and a half million.

Having completed many similar infiltrations before, Method A knows what she is doing and makes quick progress. Sticking to the shadows, she avoids any spotters and soon reaches the cargo ship bay, located close to the World Trade Center station and Gangs Hater's base of operations. Its entrance demarked by the steam rising through a manhole cover. She instructs all to crouch down as she relays a code, a series of knocks - *tap-tap-tap*. They have to wait a few tense seconds until there is a reaction, the cover wobbling as it moves up and sideways - *screech* - a large waft of sticky hot steam escaping out.

Method A calls in a low voice, 'That you sista'?

'Aye, it Keys... get inside', she instructs in an equally low voice.

The cargo bay manager looks remarkably similar to her, as if her actual sister. Less flamboyantly dressed, she wears a greyish blouse and holds a white mycelium bag packed with maggot larvae. With no further words spoken, they follow her as quietly as possible down a 30-foot long ladder, passing her cargo bay and entering into an offshoot of the PATH network - an area teeming with Papini.

Hush! Pretoria steps back, not so used to king scorpions. It scurries up to Keys, greeting her by gently stroking its large frontal claws against her wrinkled face. From the bag, Keys removes some of the larvae, which the scorpion happily devours in one go. It then turns to lead them down the tunnel, so fast that they all have to run to keep up. Going deeper into Gangs Hater's territory and into an even narrower tunnel, Pretoria is barely able to squeeze through, having to duck low as he struggles to keep up. The diversion seems to be working, their path completely unguarded - Gangs Hater too preoccupied with the battles on the edge of East Side and those in the skies.

The king scorpion leads them next through a crack in the wall, one so small that Pretoria needs the help of the others to pull him through. Their species knows the tunnels even better than the Jerseyans, every nook and cranny for miles around. On the other end, the king scorpion quietly shifts a large old-time poster frame out of the way, revealing a small room with a black metallic, spiral staircase in its centre. There, Keys feeds the king scorpion the rest of the larvae - *hush*.

It appears not all payments have been made, it's Method A's turn, looking a little glum she hands Keys the pink diamond - the hefty sum of moolah that LeSouris gave her in Gambler's Den. This could prove a price worth paying, for they have reached Gangs Hater's location without issue. They only need now to climb the spiral stairs if Keys's intelligence proves correct.

Keys whispers to Method A, 'Cannon up there, Gangs there. Watch out, I know two guards at the door always... Go get him, traitor of PATH'.

'Aye, sista'.

Method A and Keys exchange a shaka sign before parting ways. Keys returning through the crack with the king scorpion, who quietly moves the poster frame back into place, once more concealing this hidden entrance.

Method A signals to Pretoria and her guards to get ready to go upstairs, instructing, 'Follow me up, we gonna blast them Universal loving maggots'.

Her guards smile widely, showing off their silver-plated teeth, they are eager to take revenge. 'Zap them skin falls off, aye'!

Another replies, 'Gonna kill them traitors or die trying'!

'Sssh'!, Method A orders them to remain as quiet as possible, they need to catch Gangs Hater's guards by surprise or the alarm will be raised.

Gangs Hater stages his defence in an aerial defence station above them. For the price of a pink diamond, Method A is potentially meters away from uniting all Jerseyan settlements, from the 'exit' at Newark Penn station to the World Trade Center station. This would be a first, all Jerseyans under one warlord, and with it a powerful force to counter the Universal Council. One Dr VonHelmann seeks to control under the EaR, this 'New Beginning'. Only a few hours ago did it look like this achievement would be Gangs Hater's, albeit as the Council's 'puppet'. Through a sequence of tragic events and hard-fought battles, the opportunity now presents itself to Method A.

She whispers, 'Ye ready'? Pretoria nods in reply, throwing up his best shaka sign, as do the rest. 'Follow me, light-footed aye'!

Method A pulls out a large jagged knife to use on the guards by the door - her Subway Hunter too loud. Pretoria opts to guard the rear, fearful that his heavy steps will undo the other's quiet infiltration. Method A proceeds with lightning pace and soon reaches the top of the stairs, where she creeps up on the two stocky guards. Not dressed in mycelium suits like the bouncers of Gambler's Den, they wear instead the signature street gangster style of Manhattan, bright red tracksuits and bandanas. Not expecting any intrusion here, they hold their Electrozappers by their side in a relaxed manner.

Without hesitation, Method A throws her knife straight into the head of the furthest positioned guard. Slightly bluish, colourless blood trickles down his face as the others sprint to the second, knocking the guard to the floor and his Electrozapper away. Their actions so fast that a surprised and impressed Pretoria only arrives after its completion.

Method A pulls her knife out of the dead guard's head and wipes off his watery blood. Holding the Subway Hunter in one and the knife in the other, she whispers to the others, 'Zappers ready, aye'.

The door is electronically locked, blinking red it requires an eye retina scan to open. One of Method A's guards lift the semi-conscious guard off the floor and press his left eye against it. Turning from red to green. *Bing!* The door slides open, prompting all to charge in, where a shocked Gangs Hater stands by a cannon and a primitive 2D map. His guards turn sharply, drawing their weapons, but are too late to stop the plasma blasts and electric shocks coming their way. Method A stops her guards from shooting Gangs Hater next. Throwing her Subway Hunter to the floor, Method A jumps on top of him, putting him in a chokehold and her knife against his neck.

'Never mess with the Method cousins, this for Bee'! She yells at him as she punches him in his wrinkled forehead.

Ring-ring! An alarm sets off, but it's already over. Method A drags Gangs Hater to the stairs, stopping a new wave of his guards in flight - who stare back stupefied. She is now the one and only warlord of the Jerseyans.

Method A announces her victory and Gangs Hater's end, picking the tallest building in New York, 'Execution on top of One Liberty Plaza'!

Chapter 15 Take me to Church

Back on Mars, the Interrogator quickly gets to his feet and pulls out an Electroclaw from his side, an electric spiralled whip he uses for torture. It holds no rope but stings just as bad, if not worse. The Interrogator adroitly cracks the whip and catches VanWest's neck before he can react, pulling him to the floor as it spirals around. The amber stone pendant falling from his hands.

VanWest hasn't come this far to be stopped by an Electroclaw and this wretched snake-like man who yields it. Scooping up a handful of sand, he throws it into the Interrogator's face, temporarily blinding him and causing him to release the whip. VanWest charges in with a flying kick and strikes the Interrogator's upper arm - *crack, pop* - dislocating it. Not finished, he grabs the Interrogator's other arm, twisting it back and dislocating it next. *Agh!* The Interrogator drops to his knees, shrieking loudly - for once on the receiving end of a beating.

VanWest's readies to kill this wretched snake off but, as a cold wind blows through, he stops himself from delivering a final, fatal blow. Looking across at the red sand, he realises that the air is not freezing cold and that he can breathe normally. With Mars's surface being close to 95% CO_2, he and the Interrogator should have died from hypoxia already. Strangely though they have not, it is as if this area is shielded and has its own atmosphere.

Looking back at the Interrogator, he decides it may be better to not execute him. Part of the Universal Council's inner circle, who resides on the SCC-400, he could well prove useful in finding Dr King and getting back to the base. His thoughts turning to the safety of his sweet Iris. Hoping and trusting that the clones will and can protect her. Searching the Interrogator, he finds his Interspace Communicator. A device not too dissimilar to the Quantum Communicator but with one key difference, it cannot transmit through the time continuum. Cognisant of the Universal Council's threat, VanWest quickly smashes it on a rock to ensure they cannot be tracked.

Like with the icy chamber and the mural, he wonders if he is being transported to a saved itinerary of places, it's as if Mars recognises him as President Van der Westhuizen - just as the little girl did. Picking up the pendant, he grabs the Interrogator by the scuff of the neck and drags him up a slope to get a better view of their location. Where he finds a landscape very much affected by people; in front, there are hundreds of pathways cutting through a much-smoothened landscape.

Lifting the Interrogator's head up next, he asks, 'Do you know this place'?

The whimpering Interrogator shakes his head, he does not. VanWest believes him, for it does not look like the layout of any Universal Council controlled settlement. He checks his Moggle X, which returns his exact geolocation, *7 78*. Remembering that the 'Face of Mars' mountain is located in 8-77, he realises that this smoothened rock could well be that of Cydonia. Further, the numbers remind him of the tattoo on Van der Westhuizen's wrist, 777. This cannot be a coincidence? If this is indeed Cydonia, then the church he saw must be close.

VanWest checks his Quantum Communicator but there is still no message. He worries at what the reason could be; hoping it to be interference and distance rather than something worse. Not knowing how Dr VonHelmann progresses on Earth, he feels even more pressure for their mission to be a success - for Dr King's death. Entering the code *01034589X*, he sends an update: *Iris, LeSouris In Base, VanWest In Geo 7-78, Our Stone Is Amber Stone Pendant, Must Find Our Energy.*

The success of this 'New Beginning' could lie in finding the church. Although he doesn't yet fully understand what exactly lies there - *Our Stone* could unlock *Our Energy*. The President hid something under the slab in the church, he must find whatever lies there. Looking at the amber stone pendant, he figures he has a better chance to save everyone, including his sweet Iris, if he can find the church.

VanWest ushers the Interrogator to the smoothen rocks of geolocation 7-77, on what proves to be a long descent and walk. Now closer, he can see cylindrical outlines under the sand, the foundations of capsule buildings and homes. But the Interrogator starts to limp and slow, whimpering loudly. Having not slept properly since arriving on Mars, VanWest also feels tired, but he knows if he is to save Iris and LeSouris, then they must keep going. He grabs the Interrogator's by the neck once again and pushes him forward.

The crisscrossing paths become more frequent, indicating a more built-up area, the centre of this lost settlement should be close. He decides to follow the outlines of the widest path, another long trek that eventually leads him to an elevated square-shaped clearing. This could be the foundations of the church! Its outline much larger than any he has seen thus far. He notices too an indent in one section, possibly what was the entrance.

Forcing the Interrogator to his knees, he goes over, kneeling down to wipe away the red sand. As he does, the red sand changes to dark blue, there are bricks underneath! Moving more sand out of the way, he finds a stairway, the bricks leading up from the street. He remembers these steps from his vision of the church, this must be it! Looking at his pendant, he notices that it glows ever so slightly. The Interrogator's whimpering stopping, instead replaced by a silent intrigue.

La-la-la!

As he steps onto the dark blue bricks, a familiar sound returns, that from the mural. He turns around to find the little girl, Van der Westhuizen's daughter, standing beside him. She's smiling, still looking at him lovingly as if he is her father. Leaving the Interrogator behind, he follows the girl through what would have been the church's doorway. His mind-tingling, he feels its special energy flowing through him, this a divine place. An energy that momentary frees him of anxiety and worry: Dr VonHelmann, the horrors of Schuurman's lab, Iris's safety and saving Earth's citizens.

The girl leads him to the other side of the Church, to where the sermon would once have stood. VanWest looks at her, expecting some type of instruction but there is none, she only stares back at him angelically. Looking into her eyes, he remembers the distressing scene of Van der Westhuizen moving a slab. Noticing where she places her feet, he kneels down and removes the red sand. There he finds a slab, also bluish in colour like the bricks on the stairs.

Removing more sand, he realises that it is crooked in shape, different from the others around. The girl leans in to give him a kiss on the head, sending a warm feeling rushing through him, a feeling of destiny, of everything coming together for a reason. He wants to ask the girl more, but she starts to fade. He reaches out his hand, but she disappears, this time, what feels to be the final time.

He glances back to check on the Interrogator before lifting the slab, who waits, cowering in the same position. For once, it is this evil man who is afraid, not one of his countless number of victims. In this flattened, sandy ruin, there is nowhere for him to flee. Deciding he is not a concern, VanWest returns to the slab eager to find what lies beneath, his amber stone glowing brighter.

Fitting his fingers into the small gaps on either side of the slab, he heaves it up and slides it out. *Zoom!* Immediately a blue light shoots out, so strong it forces him to shield his eyes. Only for a faint, sweet humming sound to call him back. Squinting, he peers inside. At the bottom lies a decorative box, the image on its lid very much like that of the mural in the icy chamber. Though much smaller, it too misses a circular piece where the sun is - the exact size and shape of his amber stone.

Mesmerised, he brings *Our Stone* close, the key to unlock *Our Energy*. The pendant glowing brighter as he does so. Carefully, he removes the stone from its metallic frame, gently knocking it against the floor until it dislodges. The stone is drawn to it like a magnet - the sweet hum growing louder.

However, as a well-disciplined Enforcer, he stops himself. First, he needs to send an update to the others, whatever may happen could affect everyone - particularly those on Mars. But this time he finds a short message waiting on his Quantum Communicator, his mind having been too focused to have noticed it earlier. *The Fight Intense on Earth, The Commissioner Comes to Mars. If Find Our Energy In Cydonia, Use This Shield To Protect Iris.*

Realising it to be Dr VonHelmann responding to his last message, he finds it odd that the doctor never spoke of *Our Energy* or Cydonia's location before - now he reveals that he knew of both! This 'interplanetary diplomat' didn't even want to tell his own daughter that there was a shield on Mars before! Commissioner Ming implicated him in the Martian's demise, VanWest questions more and more if Dr VonHelmann really was a dissenting voice or if there is a darker truth that he hides.

Before he can unlock the box, the ground begins to shake, the red sand whipping upwards in a frenzy. As if sensing the danger, the sweet sound subsides. The face of the Commissioner in his ship flashes through VanWest's head. He jumps up and hurries over to the Interrogator, suspicious that he has something to do with this - his Quantum Communicator unlikely to have been hacked.

VanWest grabs his throat and starts to squeeze, 'Did you contact the Universal? I know you did'!

Even being choked, the Interrogator manages to reply with a mocking smile. But his small beady eyes answer VanWest's question, its shape remarkably similar to those of a Space Soldier. The Interrogator is part machine, thus making his cybernetic person traceable wherever he goes. Unsurprisingly, the Inspectors are another machine used to keep the citizens down.

VanWest releases and throws him backwards, he risks being blown to smithereens if he doesn't act quickly. Rushing back, the amber stone glowing a fiery yellowish-orange, he kneels down and without pausing inserts it into the lid of the box - the colours mixing instantly to form a bright bluish-green stream of light.

Like electricity pulsating through him, his hairs stand straight and eyes roll backwards, its energy overwhelming. Images, memories of the Martian people enter into his head, like a video upload, each tells their story.

Starting well, they speak of the great excitement in starting and establishing this settlement, building the church, raising their families, learning to communicate with one another by mind and transference. Successfully building a greener and fairer world with a breathable, less hostile atmosphere. Even minute details are included, how they switched from having a silica aerogel dome to live under and grow their food, to the wondrous green energy that arrived, turning all of Mars rich with fauna. The green energy, a technology bought to them from far away, given to them in recognition of being 'the worthy few'.

However, the stories soon become darker, decades later there is mention of aggressive humans coming from their ancestral lands, Earth. At first, offering to trade but then demanding that they become a colony, offering them a choice that reeked of virtual enslavement and servitude; arrogant and self-entitled, they demanded that the Martians mine their lands and pay tribute to them. These humans belonged to the Grand Council.

President Van der Westhuizen tried diplomacy, offering to restore the health of planet Earth in exchange for peace. The Grand Council seemed to listen at first, as he preached about 'Groene Utopie', revealing details about their green energy technology. But not long after, the memories speak of horrifying events: tricked into signing an agreement, terror engulfs the settlement; the Martians foretelling of their own impending doom, alas with no way to stop it now.

VanWest recognises it matches closely to what Dr VonHelmann showed him when only a child, the interface he showed before fleeing the moon base as a Utopian. His name becomes prominent in their stories, the Martians speaking of a leading diplomat called 'VonHelmann', then much younger and with short brownish hair. He seemed genuinely interested in regenerating Earth with this technology, he even agreed to the President's offer - also advocating for peace in its exchange. Together they signed an interplanetary agreement for the Martians to join the Grand Council as equal partners, thus forming the Universal Council.

Martians cheered as Dr VonHelmann and President Van der Westhuizen signed, with the President's wife, a pretty and redheaded woman, gifting an amber stone pendant and a book titled *Groene Utopie*. Opening up the first page, the content translated from Dutch:

Chapter 1: Living a healthy, green life
Chapter 2: Living in harmony with technology
Chapter 3: Excerpts from Philosopher Hans Ashtar
Chapter 4: Treat others as you would like to be treated
Chapter 5: Our earliest explorers - lessons learnt

VanWest realises this book to be the link between Dr VonHelmann and the Utopian religion, there is a chapter on this philosopher Hans Ashtar, who warned on the immorality of machines: its ill-use leading to the end of the Utopian dream. The woman has the same dark green eyes as the little girl, the President's daughter. But it is the woman's ring finger that catches his attention most, she wears the same bluish-green emerald ring that Iris now has.

He notices too a bald-headed man intensely watching them from the shadows. Seemingly doing his best to avoid President Van der Westhuizen and his wife, the man looks a lot like Dr King, albeit a much younger version. His long goatee black rather than white. He must have known about the President's purported psychic sense and thus kept his distance so his own plans could not be unravelled. An ability that he and Dr Schuurman would later try to harness through cloning, the reason for VanWest's very existence - him being Van der Westhuizen A1.

It was meant to be a historic deal, guaranteeing everlasting peace but it was all a sham; what would later prove to be an elaborate and fatal charade. President Van der Westhuizen's good judgment clouded by the hope of peace, maybe indeed a 'naivety' to trust that humans had goodness in them. Too keen to share his book and teachings, *Groene Utopie*.

Already the Grand Council's leading figurehead, Dr King was a most devious man. He even kept Dr VonHelmann in the dark to play his wicked ruse. In so doing, reducing the risk of the Martian President seeing what would happen next. With the creation of the Universal Council, all space neutrality rules were voided, thereafter an armada was mustered. Gifted the amber stone, the key to Mars's green energy, they were able to pass through their defences.

The Martians in all but a few moments made extinct - a genocide committed. President Van der Westhuizen's last act: to hide the decorative box, the green energy source in the church. His offer to share this technology could have helped to revitalise Earth and made more planets habitable, but for Dr King Earth's poor conditions worked to his advantage, as a way to browbeat its inhabitants into submission: to him a sickly Earth and Solar System were optimal. This is where he and Dr VonHelmann fundamentally always differed, even back then, hundreds of years ago.

Nevertheless, it was Dr VonHelmann tasked with bringing this Space armada to Mars and committing this genocide on the Council's behalf. Given only two choices: to carry out this mission or die with them. He chose to carry it out. President Van der Westhuizen could do nothing, with this amber stone key relinquished, he could not defend his Martians. But in hiding its energy source, Dr VonHelmann was prevented from finding and learning its secrets.

VanWest has reawakened this energy, the Universal Council no longer in possession of its key, the amber stone - the defence is restored. The light turns greener as it rises into the sky, spreading upwards and outwards. The blue pavement stones mirroring its light as the red sand begins to clear. The air becoming even purer, the place is slowly returning back to life.

Eeeee! The sweet sound of the box suddenly changes to a high pitch shrill, like a swarm of bees the light twists and spirals upwards. VanWest spots the SCC-300 uncloaking approximately 30 miles above the church, flanked by two auxiliary spaceships. As envisioned, the Commissioner has come. Knowing of Cydonia, the Council likely too knows why VanWest is here - they have come to stop him.

Zoom! Before the Commissioner can give the instruction for his SCC-300 to fire, the energy catches the first auxiliary spaceship, cutting through its metal and shattering it into tiny pieces. The second auxiliary ship tries to retreat - only to be struck next and sliced apart. The SCC-300 is higher up and looks able to escape, but the light moves even faster. The green energy able to recognise it as a threat races up and pulverises it on the edge of the mesosphere.

The Commissioner is dead!

The Martian's shield is active for the first time in over half a millennia, its first act to destroy a powerful Elite and high-ranking Universal Council member. News of the Commissioner's death will cause shockwaves across Earth and the solar system. A boon to the EaR. This 'New Beginning' growing even more realisable.

As the light continues to expand, VanWest activates his Quantum Communicator, sending a series of short messages, using the code *01034589X, Commissioner Dead. Send Out The News. Energy Shield Protects Mars, Geo 7-77.* Like with the shield, he assumes that Dr VonHelmann also knows about his clones - 'evil resides in there'. *My Cybernetic Clones In Lab, Trust Protect Iris And LeSouris.*

Chapter 16 Earth's Resistance

Boo-boo! As Method A brings Gangs Hater to the edge of the rooftop, the crowd jeers and calls for his death, 'Throw him off'!

Method A dangles him from the top of the hollowed skyscraper, One Liberty Plaza. The largest building situated at the westerly end of the PATH subway system. At 55 stories tall, a fall will certainly kill this warlord. Giving her the honour of becoming the one and only warlord of the Jerseyans.

From all territories, many now refugees, the Jerseyans come to bear witness. Gangs Hater will be remembered as a colluder and traitor, who chose to side with the Universal Council after breaking the PATH agreement. In so doing, allowing hundreds of thousands of Jerseyans to be murdered, including Method Bee and Rulez Haah. Rulez Haah, a dispensable pawn to the Universal Council, he was abandoned by his fair-weather ally Commissioner Ming as the EaRA arrived, much like the Enforcer Colonel Mason was in Queen Elizabeth.

Dr VonHelmann, Pretoria and Captain Kun-lee stand a few steps behind Method A, showing their support as friends of the Jerseyans. The short and bald Dr VonHelmann still presses for Method A to announce her joining of the EaR. He wants more than her just lending her ships to the EaRA, he wants her to be officially part of this alliance and go to Mars with them.

Having already received the good news from VanWest of the Commissioner's death he's keen to carry on the momentum. Taking the fight to where his daughter and the others battle. Though the mighty Space Army still outmatches them, especially without Dr King's death, his New Beginning in the present has never been more achievable.

This news already circulates amongst the Elites and several, including Marcus Vitali, have already requested clemency - asking that no reprisal befalls them. Not quite switching sides as the Huberts have done, they only offer to stay neutral and support the eventual winner. Despite this rag-tag army having far inferior ships than those commanded by Four-star General Vladimir, they know not to underestimate Dr VonHelmann. Many of their descendants have been killed in Antarctica, and the EaRA have had success in expelling the, now dead, Commissioner from Earth.

Being a shrewd man, Dr VonHelmann opts to grant the Elites their request, at least for the moment - not wanting to have their SCC class ships to contend with. Henceforth, he commands all Utopians to avoid further altercations, including the destruction of Elite owned property.

This time, Dr VonHelmann is quicker to share VanWest's news with the others, keen to demonstrate the EaR's success and put further pressure on Method A. However, he instructs them not to share this news of the Commissioner's death, that he wishes to announce himself. He seeks to maximise its gain and impact to convert the masses to Utopianism. His work thus far with these heathens only acceptable due to the Utopian's fifth commandment, *Only work with non-Utopians in order to defeat them* - the Universal Council. If the Council were to be gone, it would be a different matter.

* * * * *

'My dawgz, my peeps'!

Method A calls the attention of the Jerseyans but also that of Antarctica's citizens, the NEA able to share and relay on rebel channels without interference. This execution is to be broadcast to all of Earth, the EaR and Method A keen to capitalise on the fall of this collaborator, Gangs Hater. Serving as another rallying cry not only to the Jerseyans but also to the Free Enforcers, citizens,

Utopians and NEA. An opportune moment for the respective leaders to come to the fore.

After the death of all the Enforcer Colonels, Mathieu, Mason and Cornelius, Captain Kun-lee has become the de facto commander of the Free Enforcers. The situation so intense and violent that another vote has not yet been organised. Kun-lee, once characterised by his hesitance, now makes monumental decision after decision on their behalf: killing Master Jiang, joining the EaRA, fighting in New Jersey and next leading the patrolships to Mars.

Throwing up a shaka sign of respect, Method A announces that 'New Jersey, New York. East, West become one kingdom. Fair kingdom for all peeps'!

Cheering, the Jerseyans fire their weapons into the air as she soaks up the adulation. Waiting for them to calm, she proceeds with the execution of Gangs Hater, 'Universal loving traitor gonna die today'!

Gangs Hater lifts his bowed head to tell her to 'finish it, aye'!

Method A slaps him in the face, causing more rapturous cheering, and gives the crowd another shaka sign. The time has come, Gangs Hater balanced on the edge. This is Jerseyan culture, this is how justice is served. Those who betray PATH can only be given one sentence - death.

'Throw him'! The crowd chants.

Agh! Without another word exchanged, Method A lets go. Gangs Hater's deathly screams ending with a loud thump! Marking with it the start of Method A's 'New Beginning' and new status. The crowd throwing up their shaka signs, pledging their allegiance.

Bam-bam-boom-bang! Music starts to play, and the Jerseyans dance in her honour. She is their one warlord, their Queen. Dr VonHelmann walks up to Method A, alongside Pretoria and Captain Kun-lee, keen to discuss again her joining in EaR and coming with them to Mars.

Dr VonHelmann speaks first, 'Congratulations, Method A. We are truly happy for thy success and know this is a great day for thy peeps. Praise be'!

Method A stops him, 'What you want? You got my ships'!

Dr VonHelmann smiles, 'We want you to fully embrace this New Beginning, I believe you know the EaR to be the right PATH'.

Hitting a nerve, Method A replies angrily, 'What you know about PATH'?

Pretoria continues, 'Commissioner dead. We make to Mars, kill all Soldier. Make revenge'.

Dr VonHelmann adds, referring to the killing of Space Soldiers - including Major Chromes, 'Real revenge'!

'Nah-nah! Not Mars, I defend Earth only', Method A is still reticent to get involved in what she sees as human, 'land peeps', power plays. But more so she worries about the Utopian's leader and what he seeks.

Losing patience, the doctor points at Gangs Hater's dead body, still being beaten on the ground, to remind her, 'Without Earth's Resistance... Without our trade, thy kingdom will crumble'. Implying that she will meet the same end.

Method A retorts, 'Old, crazy doctor. You play us all. You doctor like King, aye'!

Pretoria defends, 'No, VonHelmann good doctor'!

Captain Kun-lee reasons, 'This isn't about Dr VonHelmann, neither is it about Utopianism. The Space Army is mighty. If we don't unite as one team, one squad, we will all perish! We are in this together, like it or not'.

Method A heeds Captain Kun-lee's point. Looking at the intense stare of Dr VonHelmann she realises that she has no choice, 'Gotta first be clear... Jerseyans take no order from land-dwellers. Allies to defend Earth, nothing else'!

Pretoria replies, 'Make clear'!

Captain Kun-lee says, 'Affirmative'!

'Aye, I join to Mars, become EaR'.

Dr VonHelmann smiles, as part of the EaR, her 'peeps' will be more accessible than ever before - those he seeks to convert next, 'Praise be! Thy choice is the right choice'.

Pretoria embraces Method A the NEA way, elbow and hand, sealing the alliance. As Captain Kun-lee states, her enemy is now their enemy, their fates are intertwined.

Method A walks over to her 'sista' Keys, who has been watching from the side-lines to announce her promotion to second-in-command, 'Sista, I gotta go with ships to fight Universal. I respect you... You gonna be in charge'.

Method A needs someone on the ground that she can trust. Leaving Sista Pee shocked, she answers in a squeakier voice than usual, 'My sista, boss, what'?

'You can handle the kingdom, aye'?

Giving a shaka sign, Keys accepts, 'You've got it'!

'You gonna make me proud'!

Method A turns back to the crowd, 'My peeps, we gotta go, get some real revenge on Space Soldier. To Mars'!

The crowd cheers, 'Kill the space maggots'!

Dr VonHelmann smiles widely as Method A next announces her joining, 'My peeps, we join Earth's Resistance, gonna protect Earth together - we one, E-a-R'.

Captain Kun-lee, Dr VonHelmann and Pretoria stand beside her as the crowd chant 'EaR'!

Pretoria whispers to her, 'Make ready'?

Method A nods and instructs her ships, including those once Gangs Hater's, to rise from their cargo bays and merge with the EaRA. Officially as one fighting force.

Houston communicates, 'We need to leave now. Takes 1 to 2 days to get there as a fleet'.

'Yes, make go now'! Pretoria agrees.

Captain Kun-lee notifies, 'The patrolships are ready'.

However, Dr VonHelmann is not quite done. With Earth's eyes firmly on this rooftop, he deems it the right time to reveal the news of the Commissioner's death, a calculated move to bring the spotlight back on himself and to take credit. He embellishes the success and strength of the EaR to raise his profile further and convert the masses.

'Citizens, Jerseyans! Let us embrace this New Beginning. We share great news of Commissioner Ming's dead. Praise be'! The crowd cheers as he continues, 'The Commissioner has been defeated by our faith and courage. Let us trust. Earth's resistance grows stronger, united we go forth to the red planet to destroy the Universal Council once and for all'!

Much to Method A's disconcertment - the others also surprised, he preaches, 'Embrace this New Beginning, embrace a better way of living, free of evil machines. Let us work to restore Earth's health as much as possible. Come join in Utopianism and our dream of Utopia can come true'.

Transmitting the following file to all:

Our mission is to rid the world of harmful technologies. The philosopher Hans Ashtar taught us machines would influence the way we behave and that we must resist these machines' external pressure on our moral decision-making. We must heed his message. As Utopians, these are our five commandments.

The Utopian Five Commandments:

Commandment 1. Treat all post 20th-century technology as evil.
Commandment 2. Protect planet Earth, and work to restore it to full health, including its creatures, the forests, grasslands, seas and lakes.
Commandment 3. No man, woman or child shall consume more than is needed. All resources must be evenly spread amongst Earth's people.
Commandment 4. Only recognise life-forms as those created by God. It is forbidden for man to forge and create new life-forms. This includes A.I. and cyborgs.
Commandment 5. DO NOT serve the Universal Council...

As Method A feared, he has taken this opportunity to further his own agenda, to convert the Jerseyans to Utopianism. Purposely, Dr VonHelmann did not share fully the last commandment - *and any other unelected authority. Only work with non-Utopians in order to defeat them*. As he did not want to alarm his non-Utopian allies, nevertheless he still very much believes in the latter.

Dr VonHelmann is not done, he next places the spotlight on a surprised Pretoria, declaring the NEA and Utopians are one body, 'Peeps and citizens, the NEA are the Utopians. We follow in these same commandments'! One of only a few NEA rebels, Pretoria is not a Utopian, but with these words, Dr VonHelmann forces his conversion in front of the masses, thus 'We are together, NEA-Utopians in the EaR'.

Pretoria isn't pleased, but as a pragmatic man, he also knows it is not the time to appear divided. He replies, feigning devotion, 'Praise be, let us trust in Utopia'.

The alliance is now comprised of the NEA-Utopians, and their partners the Jerseyans and Free Enforcers. Pretoria does not look at Dr VonHelmann as he pats him on the back, he communicates to Houston to beam him inside her battleship. Captain Kun-lee also leaves back to his patrolship.

Method A grabs Dr VonHelmann's arm before he goes, 'I don't trust you, crazy doctor. Jerseyan world is world of warriors. You not gonna change it'!

Dr VonHelmann only replies with a satisfied smirk as they depart to join the combined fleet of the EaRA. With only twenty cargo ships damaged in the successful incursion of Manhattan, an eclectic fleet 801 strong goes to Mars.

- *250 NEA-Utopian battleships - Houston and Pretoria*
- *300 Up-armoured cargo ships - Method A and Sista Pee*
- *250 Enforcer patrolships - Captain Kun-lee*
- *SCC-40 piloted by Lt. Colonel Wang - Dr VonHelmann*

Dr VonHelmann returns to the SCC-40, and Method A to Sista Pee's up-armoured cargo ship. The EaRA leaving together to confront and destroy the Space Army. However, Dr VonHelmann has not shared another piece of news from VanWest. Although a boon for the resistance, he does not want to explain the green energy shield. Left with the stark choice of being killed or being the killer, he committed the genocide of the Martians. Taking from them Utopianism, a bastardised version of *Groene Utopie* - adding his own commandments to lead a rebellion on Earth.

Suppressing any morsel of guilt, he justifies it all as part of the bigger picture: restoring the Utopia lost and building a new world shaped by him. His haste to Mars is not only about going to support his daughter Iris, LeSouris and VanWest; he knows he must act fast to minimise any risk of this secret being exposed. His focus is on the success of his 'New Beginning', he will do anything it takes to achieve it. Dr VonHelmann seeks to become the leader of all Utopians, ultimately of everything.

After the Commissioner's death and the energy shield expanding, VanWest's attention returns to reuniting with Iris and LeSouris. Having not heard from them or the voices of his clones, he can only but hope they are safe in the Universal Council's Martian base.

Chapter 17 A Trip Down Memory Lane

Thanks to President Van der Westhuizen's final act of hiding the energy source, VanWest has been able to reawaken it half a millennia later. The green energy shield continues to spread, revitalising the air and soil. This life source releases with it the stored memories of the Martians. So many it overawes VanWest's mind as he tries to focus on finding a path back to the Universal Council's base. He MUST find Iris and LeSouris. With no transporter, he decides his best bet is to return to where he first arrived, geolocation *7-78*.

Despite all her father has done, his sweet Iris is not to blame for any of it - unaware of his crimes. He does not know what he will say or do if he finds Iris, these memories would only destabilise the EaR and work to Dr King's advantage. Grabbing the cowering and dumbfounded Interrogator by the scuff of the neck, he drags him to his feet and forces him to walk back with him. VanWest still thinks he could prove useful, taking this opportunity to try his academy taught 'technique of overloading' to retrieve some valuable intel - anything that could help.

'How many Space Soldiers are there on Mars? Do you know where their ships are? Are their weapons in the base'? VanWest grabs his arm and twists, 'Any weapons? How many spaceships in the base'?

The Interrogator would normally not be someone easy to interrogate but, exhausted, he capitulates faster than expected, muttering at first unintelligible words, 'Old, old ship-ss, cannon-cannon on top of mount-tain'.

A cannon, this could prove useful! A notification interrupts his interrogation, there is a message on his Quantum Communicator, *My Love. In 7-78. Come Quick.* It is his sweet Iris! VanWest is overjoyed but concerned too by this word *Quick.* He messages back, *Affirmative. 01:00:00. Quick?*

VanWest waits for her reply, but there is none. With renewed urgency, he ushers the Interrogator onwards. The settlement continues to transform around them as they hurry; the fine red sand turning, rich and brown, into soil. But there are more than just memories in this ruin, he feels that they are being watched. Each capsule building in Cydonia destroyed by the Universal Council - he sees their horrific end. Not just homes, but so too the elementary school, the many high street shops, the hospital. Nothing has been deemed sacred and untouchable - all targeted.

Behind each ruin and street corner, VanWest senses spirits of the dead - whispering. This whole settlement a graveyard, the streets full of murdered Martians. Their beings are somehow tied to this green energy that grows ever larger and out from the Church. They recognise the Interrogator belongs to the Universal Council as they read his thoughts, their anger immense as he passes. A wind blows lowly through the air, within which, VanWest can hear a word being repeated, 'Moor...de...naar... moor... de...naar... murderer'.

VanWest looks at the Interrogator, his eyes are leaking an oily black liquid, and he is struggling to breathe. Having ignored his earlier whimpering, VanWest stops to help, but the spirits attack, bloody lines crisscross the Interrogator's skin. The word 'murderer' screamed by even more voices, their anger only growing. Unsure what to do, he picks him up and carries him over his shoulder as he runs towards geolocation 7-78 to escape.

Deathly howls follow. VanWest can see their final thoughts: some watching helplessly as their loved ones perish before them, others hopelessly trying to escape even though they can foresee their own deaths. Their beings forever attached to this green energy, its reactivation bringing their spirits back after hundreds of years.

The spirits though do not follow, seemingly rooted in place. But every corner and street brings new memories. Not all are terrible, the next street having been packed with market stalls, the smell and colour of their produce so vibrant and bold, many holding fruit and vegetables that he never has tasted, including sweet, red strawberries already extinct on Earth by the 24th century - unable to grow due to its radioactive and polluted atmosphere. On Mars, however, they grew in abundance.

Between the horror and the anger, he can see the happiness, the children playing on the streets that he now runs through. There is genuine warmth and friendliness between each neighbour, what a cheerful existence it once was; no crime, no Quadrotors, no locked doors, no fear. He wonders if this was Groene Utopie itself right here - these Martians had it. As he runs, he catches up with the expanding green energy, passing through it the atmosphere instantly changes to that before. The spirits are gone and the air harder to breathe - still not that of Mars but akin to Antarctica. His Moggle X updates, he has returned to geolocation *7-78*.

Hurrying back to where he came from, he senses that there is something new beyond the hill. He places the Interrogator on the sandy ground, his body having become limp and lifeless. And tiptoes to the top to get a better vantage point. The air beyond is hazy, the sand sweeping upwards into a spiral. In-between, he can make out vague objects flying lowly, coming from the direction of Alba Mons, moving like a snake in a long line - it slithers. His psychic sense magnifies the face of Lt. Colonel Omega. He comes for the Church, the source of the green energy.

Outside of geolocation 7-77, the memories quieten, and he can once again hear the clones; however, he cannot understand their words. There is no mention of Iris and LeSouris in-between their chatter. The haze clears enough for him to confirm the identity of the objects - they are Space Soldiers. Their vehicles are similar to the Enforcer's BoeingHawk gliders, those he used in Queen

Elizabeth to raid the Utopian's secret bunker under the cockroach farm. Stopping Dr VonHelmann's first attempt at a New Beginning, to change the past.

Whilst the green energy shield appears indestructible, he is also aware that this is not the 24th century anymore, the Council's spaceships have evolved, they are much more superior than those in the time of the Grand Council. The 'cannon' that the Interrogator revealed could be of critical importance.

As he looks, VanWest hears the sweet hum of the decorative box again, he turns to find that the green energy is upon him, having expanded all this way into geolocation 7-78. It quickly passes through him, the air becoming more breathable and the red sand revitalising. The spirits return with it, in this area, he sees the farmworkers and Martians that had fled the settlement. He checks on the Interrogator, not only is he dead but his eyes have been removed, his sockets hollowed - having been gouged out.

A vision crosses his mind of Lt. Colonel Omega disappearing - being erased. He turns back to find that the green energy has removed the haze in front. Curiously, he can no longer see anyone approaching. Walking to where he last saw the Space Soldier's glider, he finds that the sand here too has turned to soil, in it are minuscule red fragments. He nearly jumps back - these are remains!

Looking at his arms, he realises that there are scratch marks on his skin, though not as deep and vicious as the Interrogator's. The spirts question him, recognising him as a Martian but angered too by his presence. The little girl's scream of 'you killed us' plays in his mind. President Van der Westhuizen's openness, or 'Martian gullibility' as Dr Schuurman called it, a factor in their demise; having elected and trusted him to make the right choices, some are not so forgiving.

A broken voice calls to him, this is not from the clones, 'VanWest, Van-West'!

He turns to find from where it originates - his sweet Iris, terrified and scared, having crawled out from under a rock, 'Oh VanWest'!

VanWest runs and grabs her in an embrace, 'My sweet, are you ok'?

Iris shakes her head, 'We waited in 7-78 for you, the Space Soldiers were coming, and then they disappeared! Angry voices started shouting to me, calling me VonHelmann and a word I could not understand - moor-de-naar'.

'My sweet, do not worry, you have nothing to fear'.

As he comforts her, he hears that his name is being called again, *VanWest*, this time it comes from the clones. They are close. LeSouris comes crawling out from another rock and grabs VanWest's in a strong hug, 'My friend, praise be'!

'You too, my friend', VanWest awkwardly hugging him back. LeSouris has been left untouched by the spirits, his experience only of hiding, 'Soldiers go poof! So strange'! Keen to understand what is happening, LeSouris asks, 'This green light, you knew all along'?

VanWest! He looks up to see a small number of ships flying in the air, coming from the direction of Alba Mons. These are spaceships from a bygone era, maybe even those who attacked the Martians. Dark and clunky looking with gun turrets stuck onto its side, they resemble more the NEA's battleships than the current Universal standard. The BV73 clones must have found the disused spaceships that the Interrogator told him about. Passing through the green light, they joyfully call his name again, *VanWest*. They have overcome the remaining Space Soldiers in the base.

As VanWest helps Iris to her feet, a long black ship about half the size of the SCC-400 decloaks above them. It transports them all inside and into the command deck, the signage above the controls reads SCC-001. It is the first model, a prototype of the hyper-modern SCC series. Indeed, so effective that three hundred and ninety-nine ships more of this type were made afterwards.

A BV73 clone stands by the holomap. Mute, he seems to blank LeSouris and Iris, only able to communicate by transference to

VanWest, from mind-to-mind. The hologram switches on, showing 10 of these old spaceships stretching from Cydonia to Alba Mons. It also shows where the green energy shield has expanded to, now covering Alba Mons and the Council's base. Any remaining Space Soldier expunged.

This BV73 clone is thinking exactly what he is thinking, searching for the Space Army and Dr King, who he calls *bad man*. Anticipating a reaction. Most of the spaceships are transportation vessels, but there is one super-advanced spaceship in-between, a MajorLaser series, MLS-10, in addition to the SCC-001. Both the earliest examples of their class. VanWest had only heard unsubstantiated reports of the MLS's production. Said to the fastest and most deadly spacecraft ever created, in fact so fast that whomever it engaged would not even see their own death coming. Furthermore, the ship is very small, nimble. It holds many short-range weapons, perfect for citizen control in the settlements and larger mining colonies: very much outmatching any NEA battleship. The clone fleet is as follows:

- *8 spaceships - bygone era transporters*
- *MLS-10 (MajorLaser series) - prototype for latest and most advanced class*
- *SCC-001 (SuperCivil class) - prototype for Elite transporters*

VanWest can hear all those at the helm, a BV73 clone leading each. The BV73 piloting his ship, the SCC-001, coordinates all, so skilled he can fly it with just his mind. VanWest hugs a still shaken and confused Iris to comfort her. But she speaks only to scold him, 'So many voices, we had to run after having waited so very long for you'! Following his coordinates and message, it seems Iris and LeSouris followed shortly to 7-78 after VanWest transported there along with the Interrogator.

LeSouris takes a moment to gain his bearings and get some much-need water capsules from the ship's HyperCreator machine before coming over to speak with VanWest, 'My friend! Praise that you are alive and well! We thought we lost you in the transporter. But I ask... This green light... What is it'?

Still coming to terms with all the Martian memories, including a feeling of sadness and guilt on behalf of Van der Westhuizen, he thinks it best to not over-explain what it is: a life force, 'I found the Martian defences, an energy shield'.

LeSouris grabs his arm and elbow, the NEA embrace, 'Praise be! See why to trust in Utopia! It rewarded us'. His attention next turns to their mission, 'My friend, we kill Dr King next, yes'? VanWest nods, the doctor ever so elusive.

VanWest collects two jelly-like capsules of water and brings one to Iris, but still shaking, she is unable to hold the capsule steady and drops it on the floor. The spirits have left her bewildered, 'How did they know I was VonHelmann? Why were they angry'?

Whilst Iris knows of the Council's many horrible deeds, she does not know that her father personally carried out the atrocity on Mars. An atrocity that likely won him promotion to Head of Science shortly afterwards. VanWest decides now is not the time to discuss, and he gives his capsule of water to her. After drinking, she leaves to the ship's Hypersphere pod to get some rest and recharge. VanWest's mind turns back to Dr King, like his clones he senses him and his Space Army watching, plotting.

Alarming images shoot through his mind of Universal spaceships, pushing back the shield - a forewarning. He had worried how the shield would fair against the modern spaceships of the year 3000. He checks his Quantum Communicator for more messages, hoping that the news he shared of the Commissioner's death will rally and bring the NEA and Enforcers to Mars, but there is nothing new.

He instructs his clones and LeSouris, 'We must get in touch with the EaR as well as pinpoint the Space Army's location'.

'Already on it, my friend', LeSouris answers, the clone nods - *bad Space Army.*

LeSouris has already installed himself at the communication station, he tries to reach EaR, hacking his way through the jamming devices to get intel and reach his NEA contacts, Houston and Pretoria. VanWest also wants to know the exact size and strength of the Space Army's armada that comes. Travelling from all across the solar system and even beyond, most would have reached Mars by now. Three days have passed since their call to come together.

'My friend. You have special kind of psychic sense, yes'? LeSouris asks VanWest inquisitively. Wondering if it can help him with focusing his search.

VanWest hesitates, he has not spoken about it in detail before, 'I'm not sure what it is... In times of imminent danger, I have a feeling, sometimes visions. It is stronger here on this planet, but it is not fully under my control... It is hard to explain'.

'Do you know what lies beyond this green light? How large their fleet is'? LeSouris asks.

'I am asking about the very same question'. Sharing an ominous warning, his tone darker, 'I know that Dr King is watching us. Preparing to attack'.

'My word! This green light not suffice'? LeSouris replies, looking very worried. He had assumed the green energy shield was impenetrable, especially after seeing it pulverise Lt. Colonel Omega so quickly over the red sand.

'I do not know... We should wait under it until we get another message', VanWest advises, concealing his worry that the shield may not be strong enough. Trying to lighten the mood, he jokes, 'Try not to give them a fright with your fishy gills if you get through to Pretoria and Houston'!

'What do you mean'? LeSouris asks, having forgotten about his Jerseyan fish-like gills, a mishap of teleporting with the Magicbox after his DNA had been altered. He ripostes, 'Oh you funny man, funny, funny psychic man'!

The BV73 clones search as well - highlighting large areas of interference they believe masks spaceships beyond Mars's orbit, but are unable to confirm. LeSouris offers an ejaculatory pray before returning to his work, 'Let us trust in Utopia, all will be fine. Praise be'.

VanWest nods and leaves for a pod to have a powernap, exhausted from all he has done, seen and remembered today. However, with his mind so alert, closing his eyes only lets him see more clearly what is to come, Dr King in the SCC-400 looking at a much larger holomap containing hundreds of red dots, some of great size clustering together. His mind shifts to another spaceship, here the Space Army's Four-star General Vladimir is directing the coming together of something powerful, a great energy of their own. He points at a spot on the holomap of Mars's surface, *7-77*, that of Cydonia and the church.

VanWest rouses, distressed by what he has seen, he hurries back to the command deck. His vision confirming his fears, the Space Army targets the energy source. A rested Iris and bleary-eyed LeSouris greet him, they have been working together to make contact with the EaR, Dr VonHelmann and Pretoria. However, with little progress.

VanWest checks his Quantum Communicator, he announces 'I have news'.

He puts it on the communication station's screen, there is good news to share: The EaRA Come To Mars. Jerseyans, Free Enforcers, NEA-Utopians.

'My friends, praise be'!

Chapter 18 Our Energy

From his vision, VanWest estimates that there are close to 900 Universal spaceships, each containing onboard what must be thousands of Space Soldiers and other Universal personnel. The fleet of the Council, then Grand Council, was not as advanced when they committed the genocide of the Martians over 500 years ago. VanWest surmises that whilst the green energy shield could protect Mars of yesteryear, this could prove a far sterner test. Dr VonHelmann has not shared with him the full size of the EaRA's fleet - it will need to be substantial to offer any resistance.

VanWest strides over to the BV73 clone manning the SCC-001, 'The Interrogator told me that there is a cannon on top of the base in Alba Mons. Correct'?

He repeats *cannon, Alba Mons*. The clone is momentarily puzzled - as if to say *why* and looks at the *green energy shield.* But then sees what VanWest sees, their thoughts aligning. The chatter between the clones reach a crescendo and results in one of the older, more inept transporter ships breaking from the pack as it races back to the base in Alba Mons to man the cannon.

'The Space Army is coming'! The expanding green energy suddenly halts on the holomap. Iris calls out, 'There's a large red dot'!

VanWest and his clones know what it is. *Zoom!* A large concentrated flow of red-light blasts down from Mars's orbit and smacks into the shield. It shakes and shudders on the holomap, its colour changing from green to yellow. VanWest can visualise what is happening - multiple MLS-Arts have joined together. Somehow, the green energy resists, retreating momentarily before pushing back against the plasma build-up.

'What's happening'? A shocked Iris asks.

LeSouris looks equally puzzled, 'This is crazy'!

VanWest instructs, 'Use my Quantum Communicator and re-double your efforts to contact Dr VonHelmann and the EaRA! We need to know when they will get here'. Prompting LeSouris to upload his new hacker program into the communication station.

Iris asks, 'Where is that transporter going'?

'There's a cannon in the base, it may buy us some time'. Deciding not to sugar-coat the situation, 'But we must prepare for the worst, to engage if they break-through'.

Iris replies, 'Break-through'?

'Around 900 ships, the shield may not be able to withstand'.

LeSouris gasps loudly, 'WHHH-A-A-A-T-T-T'?

VanWest tries to calm them, 'Our ships may be weaker, but with the clones on our side we will put up a great fight... Their abilities are much more than yours or mine. They see everything, work in unison and can solve any problem in lightning speed'.

LeSouris agrees, 'Trust in Utopia. It will protect us'.

A message comes through via VanWest's Quantum Communicator and onto the communication station: *EaRA ETA 01:00:00*. Iris looks to VanWest, hoping he can confirm if the energy shield can hold this long. But he does not know.

Iris is nevertheless happy for this message, proudly replying, 'You can count on my papa'! Though there is a little hint of worry in her voice - also not knowing how many ships they come with.

'Indeed', VanWest returns a half-smile. Doing his best to conceal his own concern about seeing Dr VonHelmann after what he has learnt.

'Amazing, Jerseyans, Free Enforcers, NEA-Utopians. Praise be'! LeSouris adds.

Despite the energy shield fighting back, the red plasma of the MLS-Arts continues to build. VanWest instructs, 'Defensive positions, find natural barriers behind the green energy shield. And ready to engage'.

Iris takes charge of monitoring the holomap, helping to coordinate and look for natural defences; valleys, mountains, volcanoes that the ships can use to protect themselves. Especially for a couple that are unable to camouflage or cloak.

VanWest stresses that they must 'protect the energy source, fire at any ship that attacks Cydonia'.

'Yes, if this is Utopia, we must protect'! LeSouris answers.

Unlike Dr VonHelmann, LeSouris does not yearn for ultimate power, only that of a better life and world. One he imagines like that of 20th-century Earth, freer of immoral machines with lands full of green habitation and clean air. Having seen this green energy restore all it passed, he is even more determined to protect it. In it, he sees his dream of Utopia possible. Its importance in this 'New Beginning' stretching beyond Dr King's and the Universal Council's defeat.

VanWest encourages LeSouris to come up with some solutions to help them resist, 'This cannon and a random bunch of ships are not enough. We have to withstand their attacks for close to an hour. Any ideas'?

LeSouris smiles, his usual good humour returning, 'My friend, ideas I always have'!

'That I trust', VanWest smiles back.

The green energy shield impenetrable in the time of the Grand Council begins to retreat towards the church located in 7-77. The BV73 clone on the transporter ship has already returned to the Universal Council's base and, with some of the younger clones, works hard to break-through the blocked and fortified doors to reach the cannon. Fortunately, there are no hostiles to overcome, the green energy having earlier pulverised any Space Soldier it encountered.

LeSouris joins Iris at the holomap and switches it to battlefield mode, displaying their immediate area of the planet and identifying their 10 ships as blue dots. As the MLS-Arts bombard from above

Mars's orbit, no enemy ships have yet to approach the shield - with no other red dots showing. VanWest knows this will soon change. LeSouris uploads some intel that he has about possible enemy ships that they could encounter: a summary on their vulnerabilities and 'ideas' how to counter.

The clones keenly assimilate each piece of information as he does so. However, it includes only information on those ships that the NEA has battled with – mainly from smaller skirmishes. The MLS class ship that the clones found is very recent - the first known engagement of its type coming from Lt. Colonel Indium in Antarctica. LeSouris sets about analysing it thoroughly, but it looks indestructible.

The energy shield continues to contract, with the tip of Alba Mons piercing through it as if it were a needle. Iris informs that 'several red dots light up the holomap'. A multitude of spaceships now enter Mars's orbit and commence their assault. The clones ready for a fight, waiting in the hidden, defensive places recommended by Iris.

Zoom! Targeting geolocation 7-77, another red stream of plasma builds up and accelerates at full speed towards the energy shield, the sky exploding. It punches a hole in the shield, which is deflating like a balloon. It tries to mend, only for another plasma build-up to come. *Zoom*! Racing into it and pushing it even further back and closer to Cydonia's surface. The Universal spaceships race for the new breach.

VanWest knows that they must act quickly, and so do the clones. One of the BV73 clones responds first and uncloaks, without notifying he makes a deathly run towards the breach, accelerating towards the largest ship that attempts to pass through the second hole. The clone's transportation ship is poorly armed, but its defences are strong. His objective is to intercept and sacrifice himself in a collision, in so doing allowing the green energy time to restore. VanWest calls out *stop*, however, the clone has made his mind up.

Boom! The Universal spaceship fires a series of shots, with more spaceships waiting to enter behind. A second volley firing from the spaceship's stern finally strikes the clone's transporter ship. Albeit damaged, it manages to continue forward. VanWest can hear the BV73 saying *goodbye* before a great noise - *kaboom!* Fire spreads out and catches the spaceships queuing, inadvertently blowing a couple up. The others bidding a hasty retreat to avoid the same fate.

The shield able to restore the breach once again defends Cydonia and the energy source. The pain of the clone's death reverberates through VanWest's mind. The grief felt by so many nearly overwhelming. But it gets worse, Iris notices a disturbing development on the holomap. It is now covered by even more red dots, 200 to be precise. The Universal's spaceships are decloaking, having moved into the stratosphere as the green energy shield retreated.

The other clones call on each other to make their own final charge and confront them, but VanWest recommends caution, only 20 minutes remain of this ETA of *01:00:00*. So close, this isn't the time to be irrational and make emotional decisions. Urging *calm* as the Space Army's 200 spaceships direct their plasma firepower on the spot where the first hole was. The shield wobbles as it fights to hold firm, but it now starts to contract horizontally and away from Alba Mons.

Now manned by the clones, the cannon readies to engage as the mountain's protection is about to be completely lost. Via the SCC-001's BV73 clone and VanWest, Iris points at the holomap and directs the SCC-001 and 3 transporters with the strongest shields to assist the MLS-10 to defend the latest breach. Ordering the other 3 to stay hidden, as a second line of defence. 'Everyone put your shields to max and brace'!

'Let us trust'! LeSouris gulps. He uploads everything he has figured out on the MLS class, in particular its shield strength and speed. But he is still to figure out any weakness. The clones' ships number so few, many so much weaker, but there is still hope. The clones are top-notch fighters and fliers - 20 minutes is a long-time to withstand.

With the first hole widening, a group of spaceships try to pass through. *Boom!* The BV73 clone in the MLS ship fires to push them back, packing the firepower of at least five SCC ships its first volley destroys 4 standard class spaceships in quick succession. VanWest closes his eyes, he can see Four-Star General Vladimir's attention diverted to a force coming to Mars. He orders Lt. Colonel Indium, who leads 200 standard class spaceships now attacking, to destroy the shield before they arrive. The Lt. Colonel himself hanging back in his MLS class ship to direct.

LeSouris's intelligence is helping, the BV73 clone in the MLS-10 can pick out the weaknesses in their defences. But there are too many attacking, now 15 race to break-through and reach Cydonia. With the shield pushed further back, the cannon comes into action - *boom*. The spaceships are surprised, trying to manoeuvre out of the way, many are hit with their shields unable to defend against this powerful weapon. *Kaboom!* The sky explodes violently as a chain reaction spreads all way from the thermosphere to the mesosphere. The cannon built for planetary defence proves very effective, and its capture a massive blow for the Space Army - the Interrogator's information very valuable. The Space Army having not anticipated its use by the skilful clones.

Meanwhile, the SCC-001 and transporters come to support the MLS-10 against the incoming 15 spaceships. The MLS-10 and SCC-001 able to destroy several, but two of the BV73s' transporter ships are struck and destroyed. Their deaths echoing through the clones as well as VanWest's mind. At the cost of three dead BV73 clones, they have successfully managed to block their path. With the cannon drawing attention away, the green energy replenishes, and the hole shrinks again, slicing into pieces the remaining spaceships attacking Cydonia.

Of the 200 red dots, only 100 remain. The cannon fire does not relent, a second volley of blasts destroys more spaceships unable to retreat fast enough. Lt. Colonel Indium himself just about managing to escape in his MLS-5. His shields able to withstand.

Iris calls triumphantly to VanWest and LeSouris, 'We did it'!

However, for VanWest and LeSouris, there is a note of caution. They realise all the spaceships destroyed were of standard class. These weren't the Space Army's best ships - the MLS and SCC classes.

VanWest knows well the Space Army's guile, he surmises *a second wave is imminent*. The energy shield continues to expand back out, turning green once again, with the remainder of the clone ships regrouping underneath. The mysterious technology so advanced, it can read their Martian minds to differentiate friend from foe. LeSouris returns to evaluating the MLS class for possible weaknesses.

In addition to the MLS-10 and SCC-001, 5 clone transporters have survived with 3 destroyed. The clone fleet is now as follows:

- *5 spaceships - bygone era transporters*
- *MLS-10 (MajorLaser series) - prototype for latest and most advanced class*
- *SCC-001 (SuperCivil class) - prototype for Elite transporters*

VanWest checks on Iris, 'My sweet, how are you feeling'?

'Managing but the EaRA... Should they not be here by now'? Iris asks.

VanWest looks over to LeSouris, but there is nothing on the communication station and his Quantum Communicator. He replies to her, trying to reassure, 'Soon, do not worry'.

But as he speaks, the holomap lights up red once more, this time with 700 dots! The Space Army races into the magnetosphere, taking advantage of the still replenishing energy shield. They had all hoped for good news next - but the ETA has passed. Alas, the battle reaches its second phase. At its centre is the MLS-20 of Four-star General Vladimir, guarded by Lt. Colonel Indium's MLS-5.

LeSouris asks, 'VanWest that MLS you think General Vladimir'?

VanWest nods, he has seen his coming. They target this time the cannon on Alba Mons - no shield protects it anymore. *Zoom!* Before VanWest and the clones can react, the plasma accumulates and jolts down in a thunderous clap, smacking into the mountain and the cannon. Its reinforced metallic shell melts, turning an intense and bright red. Firing off its last couple of volleys, the cannon manages to destroy 85 ships before it is destroyed completely.

VanWest hears those inside the mountain, the BV73 and the younger clones rushing to retreat, deeper into the base. Their howls of pain so acute, many incinerated before they could get out of the cannon's chamber. The transporter stationed nearby destroyed next. The other clones want to help, but VanWest stops them - leaving the energy shield would mean certain death.

VanWest hides a lone tear as he goes over to look through the viewing portal, a distressed Iris staring at him, wondering what they should do next - it looks hopeless. Sad for the clone's suffering, their fierce defence may have all been in vain. The plasma build-up targets the green energy shield next, turning it yellow once more and pushing it back.

VanWest closes his eyes to focus, through the darkness, he sees many ships entering the magnetosphere. Long Jerseyan cargo ships, many battle-scarred. Next Enforcer patrolships and NEA battleships, spirally and pointy. But then he sees the face of Dr King, who shouts angrily to 'fire at Mad Newton'. A huge explosion following.

His Quantum Communicator activates as he reopens his eyes, and the ship's communication station displays a new message: *Revised ETA 00:00:01.*

Their delay has cost many clones their lives, but at least the EaRA has made it. The red-light and plasma build-up ceasing, the Space Army's attention is diverted to that above. VanWest is perplexed but not saddened by what he has foreseen of

Dr VonHelmann in this new vision. He tells his clones to not react to his coming - *let fate decide*. For if they are divided, they will not be able to overcome their formidable enemy, Dr King and the Universal Council.

Chapter 19 Red versus Blue

The Universal spaceships make a strategic withdrawal as they plan how to counter the arrival of the EaRA's fleet. Those on the SCC-001 gather around as a communication comes through from the Jerseyan warlord Method A, her wrinkled face broadcasted through the communication station and onto the holomap.

She greets them warmly, from inside Sista Pee's up-armoured cargo ship, 'Hey dawgz, we here to save you, kill King. Universal going down'!

'Praise be! My friend, welcome to the fight'! LeSouris hails.

Although still annoyed by their treatment in Gambler's Den, Iris decides to put it behind her and move forward. Greeting her next, as does VanWest, 'Welcome'!

'Good to see you fine skinned thangs'! Method A gives them a shaka sign of respect. Looking at LeSouris with a slightly confused look, 'Sour, your neck'?

'You not hear, I'm sexy Jerseyan now', LeSouris jokes.

'Aye'! Method A replies sarcastically. 'Gs's work'?

LeSouris face turns sorrowful, 'Yes, Gs and his contact Sista Cee'.

'What happened'? Method A asks.

'Gs die brave death, help us to base', LeSouris replies. Thinking it best to omit that under torture he revealed their location at Sista Cee's office.

VanWest does the same, 'Gs helped us. He's a hero. Schuurman is gone, the Commissioner and the Interrogator all with his help'.

'Many peeps, cousin Method Bee killed. We gonna get revenge on Soldiers. Kill them all', Method A replies.

'We also', Iris replies.

Method A asks next, 'That bluish-green stuff? Who pilots your ships'?

Iris finds it hard to give a clear answer to her questions, not understanding it well enough to explain, 'The energy shield, the ships, they are... well... of VanWest'!

The BV73 clone introduces himself with a bow, drawing a smile from an intrigued Method A. Seeing the resemblance, she asks, 'Ah, you VanWest son, aye'?

Before VanWest can reply, LeSouris jumps in. Knowing Method A best, he decides against clarifying, 'My word, you have no idea! VanWest have many, many sons'!

VanWest returns an awkward smile.

'Respect dawg! Impressive'! Method A replies.

In New Jerseyan culture, having a lot of children is revered. With the radiation poisoning of the 21st and 22nd century, many humans, as well as Jerseyans, became infertile. Those able to procreate were essential to their survival and the eventual evolution of the new homo sapiens, which some derogatorily refer to as the 'Jerseyan mutants'.

Method A continues, on the way to Mars, 'some crazy cyborg ships fight us. Space heated'!

Iris updates on their own situation, 'Four-star General Vladimir leads over 550 spaceships, many of the most advanced class. We had help of a defensive cannon on Mars and the energy shield, but they destroyed the cannon'.

Method A replies ominously, 'About 100 'cyborg ships in space'! She asks again, 'Energy shield'?

As she speaks, Sista Pee brings their long and narrow cargo ship through Mars's magnetosphere. As the holomap updates with 275 new blue dots. All Jerseyan up-armoured cargo ships, though many battle-scarred after skirmishes along the way - with 25 lost. It seems that with the Space Army focused on destroying the energy source, there has yet to be a full-scale engagement between the two sides.

Before Iris and LeSouris can answer her last question, another transmission comes in, projected on the holomap is Pretoria, Houston and Dr VonHelmann. And, to VanWest's personal delight, Captain Kun-lee.

'Make great to see you', Pretoria greets with a big smile.

As does the NEA's top pilot Houston, 'Hi there, boys and girls'!

Iris is excited to see them all, 'My dear friends, so happy that you have come'. She then asks her father, 'Papa, what took you so long'?

'My love, so glad you are safe. We came as quickly as possible, doing our best to avoid a direct confrontation with the Space Army'.

500 more blue dots appear on the holomap, entering through Mars's magnetosphere. Many of the patrolships and battleships hold their own scars, these from the fight to save Queen Elizabeth. The EaRA's numbers having grown substantially after Method A and the Jerseyans joined the alliance. With the clone ships, the EaRA has:

- *250 NEA-Utopian battleships led by Houston - Pretoria*
- *300 Up-armoured cargo ships led by Method A*
- *250 Free Enforcer patrolships led by Captain Kun-lee*
- *SCC-40 piloted by Lt. Colonel Wang - Dr VonHelmann*
- *5 Transporter spaceships piloted by BV73 clones*
- *MLS-10 piloted by BV73 clone*
- *SCC-001 piloted by BV73 clone - VanWest, Iris, LeSouris*

Dr VonHelmann rallies all gathered, 'Praise be! Today is a day of reckoning, a watershed in time. We are gathered here for this New Beginning. Victory is within our grasp! Let us trust and go take thee'!

'Good to see you, old man. Utopia is here. This green light'! LeSouris proclaims.

Dr VonHelmann returns a nervous smile, 'Indeed'.

The BV73 clones chatter amongst themselves again about killing Dr VonHelmann – many wanting to direct him into the green energy thinking it will recognise him. VanWest closes his eyes to reason with them once again, telling them Dr King is a *bad man, worse*. Explaining as clearly as possible, they need to be pragmatic and put any feelings of revenge to one side.

Captain Kun-lee addresses next, 'VanWest, we the Free Enforcers join you. We come to avenge those lost, Colonel Mathieu and Captain Dell among them'.

VanWest hadn't received news of their deaths but isn't surprised, saluting and then replying, 'Their deaths will be honoured'!

Captain Kun-lee pauses for a moment, addressing VanWest specifically, 'I did not act in the Colosseum. Here on Mars, I act decisively. As part of this New Beginning, part of the EaRA'.

'Captain, glad to have you. Your piloting skills are second to none. Thank you for respecting the Code of Honour. You have paid it back and more. I count you as my friend'.

Captain Kun-lee smiles, 'Friend, yes'! A term not common in the year 3000 among Enforcers, this word symbolic of their 'New Beginning'.

Pretoria replies heartily, 'We make all friends'. Putting his own ill-feelings aside, in particular, that of VanWest's time as an Enforcer, where he oversaw the NEA rebel leader's death in ColaBeers and the subsequent slaughter of many innocent citizens.

A mass of red dots sweeps towards the blue dots on the holomap. 450 spaceships of the Space Army mount their attack. The remainder targeting the energy shield around Cydonia.

Seeing this, Iris interrupts them and says, 'Proceed with haste through the green light. It protects'.

But Dr VonHelmann objects, 'We have the numbers, let us fight here'. A confirmation to VanWest that he fears the energy shield; no longer in possession of *Our Stone*: the amber stone pendant or the emerald ring, he must know he will be targeted by it. However, in doing this, he risks the EaRA's motley fleet of ships;

much less advanced, the protection of the shield could have given them the edge.

'Papa, is that wise'?

Dr VonHelmann ignores her, 'Let us make our stand'! Pretoria and Kun-lee follow his lead and nod in agreement.

The EaRA's fleet organises into an arrow formation of three rows, the largest ships with the most powerful offensive weapons at its core, and those ships with the best defences, be it reinforced armour or forcefields, at the front. The SCC-40 and Dr VonHelmann staying well protected in its centre.

They must battle 550 Universal spaceships, red dots.

- *MLS-20 - Four-star General Vladimir*
- *MLS-5 - Lt. Colonel Indium*
- *40 MLS class - operated by various higher-ranked Space Soldiers*
- *508 Standard class spaceships - operated by lower-ranked Space Soldiers*

LeSouris shares his most up-to-date intel with the EaRA as Iris warns, 'Beware of their MLS class ships, they pack the firepower of 5 SCCs'.

Houston acknowledges, 'Yep, we fight one over Queen Elizabeth. They sure are tough'.

As expected, Lt. Colonel Indium leads the frontal attack with the MLS class spaceships, the Jerseyans more defensive ships taking the brunt. Unable to manoeuvre out of the way, 25 are destroyed in quick succession and a further 10 rendered inactive. Houston and Kun-lee react by moving their ships out of the defensive arrow to counter, doubling up on each MLS ship, in so doing allowing the damaged ships to escape through the stratosphere and into the green energy. Dr VonHelmann still keeping his distance.

Watching the General's 99 spaceships attacking the energy shield, the BV73 clones spot an opportunity, like a game of chess they see that the king is exposed - the Four-star General. They do not hesitate as they race through the green energy to intercept, outnumbering his ship at seven to one. Their adroit flying skills and quick reactions help them elude and dodge a series of powerful blasts. Arrogantly, the Four-star General does not request support, his spaceship virtually indestructible he sees no need.

The clones sense that this highly prized scalp could destabilise the remainder of the Space Army and give the EaRA a much-needed morale boost; another henchman of Dr King's dead, his powerbase further eroded. The BV73 on the SCC-001 looks at LeSouris, having seen that he has hacked the Universal Council's Wiki. Having worked hard to find any weakness in the MLS class, he has decrypted a file tagged *Advances in Cold Fusion.*

'The engines are nuclear powered, cold fusion'! LeSouris announces his 'eureka' moment.

For VanWest, it immediately triggers the memory of the Aramco Power Station in Queen Elizabeth, its nuclear reactors and wet cooling chambers. 'So, the MLS must have coolers onboard like any other, correct'?

LeSouris nods with a big smile, he understands nuclear propulsion engine technology well enough to spot a potential weakness; the MLS class ships vent hydrogen gas to cool down periodically, in so doing disrupting their shields. A plan starts formulating in his mind, if the Four-star General brings his reactors to full power for a long enough duration without venting then the hydrogen levels will pass 4%. When the MLS does vent - at this point, it would be highly flammable and significantly weaken its rear shield.

'My friends, I've dastardly plan'! LeSouris explains with a sly smile, 'We cause this MLS to fire nonstop, say four minutes till hydrogen level at 4%, then bam! When it vents, we slap General's ship on backside'!

The BV73 clones assimilate his words, understanding enough - the MLS-20 ship needs to fire at them nonstop for a whole 4 minutes. But LeSouris's plan brings great risk; it's equivalent to dodging 8 or more quick-fire rounds, in fact, it is a kamikaze mission. The SCC-001's BV73 clone zooms in on the holomap, bringing up the MLS-20 in 4D form to run a simulation, the result is positive. The game of chess continues, the clones working as knights to draw out the king - Four-star General.

The clones immediately enact LeSouris's plan, VanWest updating his Moggle X, counting down from *00:04:00*. The BV73 ships divert their power to their thrusters to draw fire as they fly by the MLS-20.

It takes the bait! Firing furiously out, with so many shots in quick succession it waits to vent - the hydrogen level rising in the cooling chambers of its reactors.

LeSouris looks at VanWest and Iris and says, 'Today we see what fate brings us'.

'It better work'! Iris replies.

The SCC-001 swerves violently as it joins the fray. With the power of the stabilisers and life support diverted, the trio must hang on with little oxygen; less of an issue for the cybernetic clones. It's a risky move, but the EaRA will lose if they do not try, already struggling against the onslaught by Lt. Colonel Indium and 450 spaceships. The energy shield also struggles, ceding ground to the 99 standard class spaceships that attack.

VanWest closes his eyes as a disturbing vision shoots through his mind. That of a BV73 piloted transporter exploding while the Four-star General laughs at its demise - 'Such primitive ships'. The rest of the clones will have seen this too, some knowing they will die today. But they do not waver. This *bad man* must go.

Boom-boom! The BV73 clones do not slow, managing to outsmart the MLS-20's first few volleys with a combination of defensive sequences as the timer runs to *00:02:00*. But the transporters cannot outrun the latest salvo, firing at full tilt the MLS-20 catches its target this time. *Kaboom!*

Over the next minute, two other transporters are picked off, VanWest feeling each death cutting through him like a dagger. Of the BV73s clones, only 4 remain in this battle. With so many killed, there will be no second chance if this risky plan does not work.

Having been so focused on all that has happened, it suddenly dawns on VanWest that one BV73, the eleventh clone, and Van der Westhuizen A103 are unaccounted for. The scene though is too tense to ask the others.

The timer hits *00:00:30* with the Four-star General having figured out their manoeuvres, another transporter ship is blasted out of the sky before the countdown hits *00:00:00*. The remaining two BV73s, piloting the SCC-001 and MLS-10 respectively, have only this moment to strike as the MLS-20 stops firing to vent.

Aiming for the MLS-20's rear shield, the BV73 clones switch all power from their thrusters to the weapon systems. *Kaboom!* A massive explosion follows, the flammable hydrogen interfering with the MLS's shield, it is blown to smithereens. The leader of the Space Army is dead! LeSouris's smart hack and risky idea having brought them victory.

But they are not out of danger, the blast radius is so large that a fragment hits the SCC-001's thrusters and cuts its power. Unable to propel itself, they all brace themselves for a crash landing as it begins gliding down, the holomap shows them coasting towards the MC-6 region known as Utopia Planitia. Unfazed, Iris hurries to send a communication broadcast to all in the EaR to confirm that the Space Army's head is dead. This is their biggest scalp.

The Universal spaceships fall back to regroup. Command falls to the lower-ranked cyborg Lt. Colonel Indium, with Major Chromes now second-in-command. Both perturbed to find out that their advanced spaceships are not indestructible. Fearing the SSC-001's crash, LeSouris sends all instructions on how to target the MLS class.

Fortunately, the green energy slows the SCC-001's descent and carries them gently to the ground, landing with a small thump. Albeit a great triumph, VanWest feels so much sadness at all who died.

He looks up to find Dr VonHelmann's face on the SCC-001's holomap, he is celebrating, 'Praise be to Utopia! The Space Army demoralised, their MLS spaceships flawed, victory is within our grasp'!

*****

Defeating the mighty Space Army has never been more achievable. With the battle recommencing, the tactic of targeting the MLS's weakness is paying off, the red dots on the holomap falling rapidly to 403, lower than the blues at 497. The green energy too has risen, passing through Mars's stratosphere it traps many of the Universal spaceships between it and the EaRA's fleet.

The blue dots:

- *158 NEA-Utopian battleships - led by Houston - Pretoria*
- *155 Up-armoured cargo ships - led by Sista Pee - Method A*
- *182 Free Enforcer patrolships led by Captain Kun-lee*
- *SCC-40 piloted by Lt. Colonel Wang - Dr VonHelmann*
- *MLS-10 piloted by BV73 clone - VanWest*
- *SCC-001 partially active (not flying) - BV73 clone, Iris and LeSouris*

And the red dots:

- *MLS-5 - Lt. Colonel Indium*
- *MLS-25 - Major Chromes*
- *18 MLS class - operated by various high ranking Space Soldiers*
- *383 Standard class spaceships - operated by lower-ranked Space Soldiers*

The MLS-10 lands beside the SCC-001, coming to collect VanWest to resume their search for Dr King. VanWest can feel his presence, and that he readies to attack again. He fears another deadly strike is imminent, much like with the destruction of the cannon that killed so many of his clones. But before leaving the

SCC-001, he notices on the holomap that Captain Kun-lee's patrolship is locked in a deadly duel with Major Chromes on the edge of the green energy shield.

A communication comes through, 'One-on-one with Major Chromes, requesting support, copy that'?

'We make come', Pretoria and Houston fly to his rescue. VanWest is impressed to see rebel and Enforcer working together so well.

LeSouris connects with Kun-lee and Houston, going through the instructions he sent earlier, 'Make MLS fire nonstop 4 minutes. Then hit cooler vent, near the engine and thrusters - very combustible this radioactive hydrogen gas residue. Praise be'!

Method A joins the attack keen to revenge Method Bee, 'Gonna blast space scum out of sky for my cousin'.

Albeit the weapons of her cargo ship are less powerful, Sista Pee readies to fire on her signal. It seems the Space Army is yet to realise their vulnerability as Major Chromes attacks, firing full pelt he soon causes his propulsion engines to max out and vent the hydrogen. Captain Kun-lee skilfully managing to avoid getting hit.

'Fire'! Jerseyan, Free Enforcer and NEA-Utopian fire all weapons.

'Yeeha'! Houston shouts.

Boom! The shots hit their target and turn the MLS spaceship into an inferno, killing Major Chromes. Another major casualty for the Space Army.

'Woohoo! That space roach is toast'! Captain Kun-lee celebrates. Thanking the others for coming to his aid, 'I give honour'.

'You're welcome', Houston replies.

Method A congratulates as well, 'Aye, big moment... My cousin's killer blown up'!

Their victory is short-lived. Another MLS spaceship emerges and fires, it's Lt. Colonel Indium, the eradicator of Ellsworth and killer of Enforcers Colonel Mathieu and Captain Dell. Hitting Sista Pee's cargo ship, whose defences are already weakened, the shot tears through the command deck. Method A throws herself to the floor, but Sista Pee isn't so lucky, the flames incinerating her.

'Sista'! Method A screams.

Before the ship explodes, Captain Kun-lee manages to put a transportation lock on, beaming her over in the nick of time. Lt. Colonel missing out on another scalp. Houston is quick to react, drawing the Lt. Colonel's attention away as she dodges a series of shots. He too has yet to fully realise the fatal flaw in the MLS's design and falls into the same pattern of maxing out the reactors. Even as he diverts all power to the rear shields, Captain Kun-lee reacts quicker, firing at the vent - *kaboom!*

VanWest does wonder how such advanced spaceships could have been built with this fundamental flaw. Another oversight by the Head of Science, Dr Schuurman - the other being his inability to control the BV73 clones. This critical weakness has cost the Space Army their leadership; Major Chromes, Lt. Colonel Indium and Four-star General Vladimir all dead.

Victory is within touching distance as the remaining spaceships are now in full retreat. With them gone, the green energy now covers the entire stratosphere, causing an uneasy Dr VonHelmann to edge upwards and further from the safety of the main part of the fleet. VanWest notices that his hands are shaking.

Instructing all, 'The fight is not over, we must continue to watch for Dr King. Victory will only be ours once he is dead'.

Chapter 20 Groene Utopie

As VanWest leaves his damaged ship to join-the BV73 clone on the MLS-10, Iris stops him outside to give him a kiss and a hug. With the green energy revitalising Utopia Planitia, the air here is so sweet and warm. The melting ice caps filling the basin with water. This place aptly named, it translates as the plains of paradise. A newer and greener world is materialising all around them.

Iris leans down and picks up a handful of mud, picturing this place as their new home, she offers a poem, 'My love, let us bless this moment'.

'My sweet, Emily Dickinson again'? VanWest replies with a smile.

To make a prairie,
it takes a clover and one bee.
One clover, and a bee.
And revelry.
The revelry alone will do,
if bees are few.

VanWest kisses her once more, 'This will be our Groene Utopie'!

Iris takes off her emerald ring and hands it to VanWest, 'My father asked for this, I'm not sure why but it is important'!

VanWest knows why but says nothing - the BV73 clone transports them inside. The MLS-10's command deck is much more spacious, its controls and holomap sleeker and more intuitive. With a BV73 at its helm, its deadliness is amplified even further. The patrolships and battleships chase down the remainder of the Space Army, with only 300 spaceships, they continue to retreat.

As VanWest looks at the holomap, he sees the same vision as before, Dr King laughing as a flash of intense red-light shoots down.

A panicked voice breaks his vision, LeSouris's shouting through the communication station, 'Attention! I locate the doctor! Look at your holomap, zoom out, there is small energy signature outside of Mars's orbit... Huge build-up of energy. My word'!

'What Sour'? Method A reacts, commanding the Jerseyans from another up-armoured cargo ship.

LeSouris replies, even more stressed, 'Get to the shield! A trap. Doctor sacrifices fleet to trick everyone'.

A glance at his BV73 clone confirms his vision. Knowing who the target is, VanWest hesitates to reply and intervene - maybe all the doctors dying today is fated.

Having instructed to go higher to stay away from the green energy shield, Dr VonHelmann's SCC-40 ship is exposed from above, he shouts at his pilot Lt. Colonel Wang to 'power up thy shields'!

Zoom! A long line of intense red plasma thumps down from space and smashes into the SCC-40. The beguiler Dr King has played them all, using his Space Army as bait, he targets the self-appointed leader of the EaRA.

As if addressing VanWest, Dr VonHelmann's last word crackle through, 'For-give-ee'. *Kaboom!* VanWest watches his ship blow up, feeling nothing as he watches him perish. His death in the end like those he massacred in Cydonia.

'Papa'! Iris screams.

'Make peace', a shocked Pretoria replies next.

'May he ascend to Utopia', LeSouris gives a short prayer.

'Divert all power to shields'! VanWest reacts to ensure others in the EaRA do not meet the same fate. The Space Army's retreat halts; the spaceships are coming back to engage.

For many of the EaRA's ships it is as perilous to retreat to the green energy shield as it is to advance, they will be struck if they turn and run.

Iris takes central command of the EaRA, conferring with LeSouris, she instructs, 'My father's death will not be in vain. Method A holds off the Space Army's remaining spaceships on Mars'. Instructing the rest of the fleet to fly to space; 340 ships belonging to the 'Free Enforcers and NEA-Utopians go get that evil roach, Dr King'!

'Aye'! Method A acknowledges, not sad to see the doctor dead.

Captain Kun-lee adds, 'We will kill him in Dr VonHelmann's honour'.

Before the intense red-light can envelop them next, Pretoria and Captain Kun-lee divert some power back to their thrusters to make an audacious fight back. A deadly 1000-mile climb to reach Dr King and his long-range bombers, the MLS-Arts. Many of them won't make it but staying here isn't an option.

Zoom! Wreckage litters the sky as ship after ship is struck. The Free Enforcers patrolships and NEA battleships do their best to outmanoeuvre, but many have been badly weakened from earlier melees. Despite the losses, the pilots bravely persist, as the old adage says fortune favours the brave, with Dr King's death the end of the Universal Council. This 'New Beginning' sought by all in the EaR.

Under the unrelenting bombardment, VanWest barely makes it through Mars's orbit. Only his MLS-10 and 99 other ships have made it thus far. Across them, Dr King's SCC-400 is flanked by 50 spaceships: 30 hyper-fast SC Max fighters and 20 long-range MLS-Arts. In real terms, they now outnumber the EaRA's much-dwindled fleet two to one, the Universal Council's remaining ships much more advanced. But one thing VanWest has learnt is to never put too much faith in odds, as with the Universal Games, he has proved them wrong time and time again. Captain Kun-lee, Pretoria and ace pilot Houston have also made it. Their ships poised to engage, with their offensive weapons armed.

- *MLS-10 - BV73 - clone and VanWest*
- *45 Battleships - Houston and Pretoria*
- *54 Patrolships - Captain Kun-lee*

LeSouris and the BV73 clone have meanwhile upgraded the holomap to show the red dots, with Iris calculating the optimal engagement strategy, 'Captain takes on the SCC-Max fighters, Houston the MLS-Arts. VanWest the...

VanWest finishes, 'Doctor'.

Kun-lee agrees, 'Affirmative'!

Houston answers, 'I'll do my best'!

'We make quick', Pretoria adds.

There is no time to discuss. Iris places those with the best shields against the MLS-Arts and the nimblest against the SCC-Max fighters. Iris and LeSouris next contact VanWest alone, she has a plan on how to defeat Dr King, reminding them all of her infiltration into Ward B on the moon base, 'Remember the holoscreen when I arrived as Nurse Rose'?

'You want me to try this on the SCC-400... Transport inside'? VanWest replies.

Iris asks LeSouris, 'Can you do it again'?

LeSouris shakes his head, the security is too tough, 'My word, this is too much. I have teleportation sequence but security impossible... I try before, security recognise your blood, your status. Not just an Elite, you must be authorised for such ship'.

VanWest answers, transmitting its data, 'Colonel Cornelius's diamond chip, it has his security codes, he piloted the SCC-400. He was its Elite guard'.

LeSouris analyses, 'It may recognise Colonel's chip, let you through... Only you'. The BV73 clone comes over to LeSouris to help. 'But SCC-400 has many fail-safes. It's risky'!

VanWest answers, conversing with the clones, 'BV73 can help alter the security triggers, make it look like I am the Colonel for long enough. Works for you'?

LeSouris returns a nervous smile, 'My friend, let us trust... Let us try'!

There isn't much time, the MLS-10 flies full speed to reach Dr King, flanked by Houston and her battleships.

'Stay sharp, shields and thrusters', Houston advises.

The Free Enforcers patrolships split off to the engage their overmatched foes, the 30 SCC-Max light fighters. As the 20 MLS-Arts ships reposition for short-range combat, targeting the battleships and MLS-10. Iris updates Houston, the instructions to buy time for VanWest to transport onto the SCC-400 and kill Dr King.

The Jerseyans more defensive, up-armoured cargo ships may have been better suited for this mission, but the NEA-Utopian battleships are faster. At short range, the intense red-light of the MLS-Arts ships becomes wider and less focused, like a machine gun, it spreads its ammo across. Those battleships most damaged and battle-scarred are quickly neutralised, but Houston does well to lead defensive sequences and get a dozen of her fleet to the halfway point.

Not built for short-range combat, the force of the MLS-Arts' red-light becomes less intense on the final stretch. Houston instructs her battleships to come together and combine their forcefields.

Boom! Dr King surprises by joining the fight, sending a number of powerful shots to penetrate their shields, destroying 2 on the flank. Only eight battleships remain active, in addition to the MLS-10, but by Dr King coming to fight he is now in transportation range. Dr King turns his attention on the MLS-10, but the BV73 clone is up to the task, deploying a series of skilful manoeuvres to keep them from being struck. Removing a silver plasma rifle from the emergency weapon's panel, VanWest heads for the transporter. However, before he transports, a distressing communication comes in, Pretoria's and Houston's luck has run out, smoke billows from their battleship.

This is their end, Pretoria's final words, 'Make world good'.

Kaboom! VanWest hears Pretoria and Houston's ship explode, mouthing back 'I won't let you down'.

It's now or never, the BV73 clone activates LeSouris's adapted hacker sequence to allow VanWest to teleport through to the SCC-400's holomap, located on the command deck. If he fails to rematerialise, this will not only be his end, but the EaR's too.

Iris sends a communication, 'My love, my brave VanWest, I trust in you. We will be together in Utopia'.

LeSouris commences the countdown, 'Ready in 3, ...2, ...'

VanWest transports across space itself, passing through the SCC-400's shields without issue. He arrives through the holomap and stumbles onto the floor of the command deck.

'VanWest'! A much-shocked Dr King stands in front.

Two Elite patrol androids burst forward to intercept him, careful to not to hit any critical equipment as they fire their weapons. VanWest gets to his feet and leaps behind the communication station for cover. Armed with his silver plasma rifle, he knows he must act fast before more support can arrive and decides on yet another risky solution. Switching his weapon to maximum power, he throws it in the direction of the androids, who instinctively shoot to destroy - *bang*! It explodes, frying them with it.

VanWest takes cue and races out, charging at Dr King, but before he can reach him a large, powerful man intercepts him and tackles him to the ground. VanWest immediately recognises him, it's Barys! His purple eyes still dilated. He last saw his Enforcer squad member suspended in a liquid behind an opaque red panel, whilst walking down a corridor of the Universal's moon base. What would prove to be his first face-to-face meeting with Dr King. Captain Barys looks enraged, like a bull who has seen red. His body veiny and muscular, it appears that he has been heavily drugged.

Barys pushes VanWest down, wrapping his hands around his neck and squeezes. VanWest tries to escape but cannot. Struggling to breathe and keep conscious, images flash through his mind, the happy sight of Iris gently rowing towards him in a wooden boat as he stands on the deck of an aluminium plated house holding a young child. The child waving enthusiastically as she approaches, the woman calls to him, 'VanWest, VanWest, my love, wake up'.

VanWest rouses, with his last morsel of strength, he punches Barys as hard as he can into the side of his head. So strong that it forces Barys to release him from his deathly grip. VanWest then throws him to the left-hand side and jumps back to his feet, following up with a kick to Barys's face that sends blood splattering across the floor. Barys manages to swing his fist once more, which VanWest ducks to return a second kick, this time into his chest. Barys falls backwards, knocking his head against the cold hard floor.

As VanWest climbs on top and wraps his hands around his neck, in the corner of his eye he spots Dr King watching, looking oddly gleeful. The doctor could have killed him, but instead waits for him to finish off one of the closest people VanWest has ever known, his squad member that has been by his side all the way from his Enforcer academy days to the Universal Games. Indeed, Barys has rescued him on so many occasions that there is more than honour between them, this is his 'friend', his best friend.

'Do it! Kill him. Come on my boy'!

Dr King wills him on, holding an Electroclaw in his hand. Before VanWest can react, the whip latches around his neck, just like the Interrogator did in the red sands of geolocation 7-78. Here though there is no sand to throw in Dr King's eyes.

'Kill him! Or I will you'! Dr King orders. Still trying to control VanWest; his need to dominate hasn't waned.

'Go roach yourself'! VanWest resists, causing the Electroclaw to tighten further and drags him off Barys and along the floor.

'Lest I need to say, you are a failure! Weak just like Van der Westhuizen. It's in your DNA. Lest I say we tried, yes we tried'! Dr King admonishes him, just as Commissioner Ming and Dr Schuurman, blaming his Martian 'naivety'. The Electroclaw causes VanWest's neck to redden and his face to turn purple.

'Stop! Stop'! The words shouted are not VanWest's.

Back on his feet, a bloodied Barys charges at Dr King and knocks him to the ground, his 800-year-old head snaps back and cracks as his Electroclaw is knocked away. Barys follows with a vicious punch that smashes into his skull - *crack*, the sound echoing loudly. With the doctor lying paralysed, VanWest staggers over to pull Barys back.

Waaahhhh! The familiar sound of a siren fills the SCC-400. With more of his guards soon to arrive, it MUST end now. VanWest has a final farewell message, in particular for 'Van der Westhuizen's daughter! The genocide of the Martians. This is for them'.

He delivers a final deathly blow to Dr King's head.

Finally, it is over, the King is dead and with it the Universal Council. An injured VanWest staggers over to the communication station and contacts the remaining spaceships as well as the EaR to share the news. The red-light outside fades, the much-diminished Space Army standing down - Earth's Resistance victorious.

Chapter 21 The Present

Gazing into Iris's eyes, VanWest takes her left hand and slides her emerald ring gently back onto her finger, 'I do'. Following the traditional Martian customs, he has learnt so much about over the past several months, this ring seals their eternal bond in marriage.

A smiling LeSouris, still sporting fish-like gills, officiates their wedding. He nods at Iris and then VanWest, 'Praise be to Utopia! You may now kiss the bride'.

A chorus of claps and cheers come from those in attendance as VanWest kisses Iris on her lips. The loudest those from VanWest's best men, his one-time Enforcer squad members, Colonel Kun-lee and Lt. Colonel Barys, elected the leaders of the Free Enforcers. Crowding behind are VanWest's cyborg clones, dressed in a variety of different coloured jumpsuits that differentiate each class. They are excited to witness their 'father' getting married to their new 'stepmother' Iris, recently made President of Mars. The two remaining BV73 clones from the battle are among them, one supports a black mycelium jacket on top of his jumpsuit, starting to show his individuality.

Lining the walls of Utopia Planitia's Great Hall are the digital 3D images of the EaR's fallen comrades, placed in their honour and memory. So many Free Enforcers, Jerseyans, Martians, and NEA-Utopian rebels died so others could live and thrive in a world free of tyranny and oppressive machines. Theirs the greatest sacrifice. In the centre is Colonel Cornelius, his sacrifice a catalyst for the formation of the Free Enforcers, who switched sides in favour of the EaR. And beside him, those of Pretoria and Houston, the leader of the NEA in Queen Elizabeth and their most decorated pilot, who helped defeat Dr King.

The 'New Beginning' is in full swing. The clones reside with Iris and VanWest in a new settlement on the banks on the great lake of Utopia Planitia. White-flowered water lilies decorate its surface; the water clear and drinkable. Their lives a far cry from the dank lab of Dr Schuurman under Alba Mons. Many having grown to the size of adults, though still mentally the age of young children they now attend school to learn more about emotional intelligence as well as how to speak.

LeSouris has won an election of his own. Becoming President of the EaR in Antarctica, he has come to Mars not only to officiate this wedding but also to sign a new *Interplanetary Space Neutrality Agreement* and the *Three Nations EaR Bill,* alongside President Iris of Mars and, the newly titled, Queen Method A of New Jersey and New York. The Queen having a limited role in the EaR only for planetary defence and order. With new trading routes having been established.

Gone are the Quadrotors and patrol androids, the Free Enforcers led by Colonel Kun-lee remain to help police Antarctica. They extend not the cold force of the law but work with local communities and government officials to help keep settlements safe, stopping the flow of the super-addictive drug known as Liquid Blue - thereby reducing crime levels. Like many Free Enforcers, VanWest suffers terrible nightmares, his own that of Dr Schuurman over the sacrificial stone sermon, with the tiny hearts of his clones. He now chooses to live his life on Mars with Iris and build a new Martian society.

Whilst a number of Oligarchs, Elites including Bramsovica, have gone into hiding, others not involved directly in any genocides or massacres, such as the Huberts and Marcus Vitali, have been allowed to repent. Participating in the building of free economies, which provides for enterprise and competition. Further, they support a green economy, with polluting spaceships banned from entering Earth's atmosphere and mining operations significantly cut back. Their descendants have become 'ordinary' citizens like any other with no fewer or greater privileges.

Mining colony prisoners have been welcomed to both Mars and Earth. Great care is being taken to help them to mend, but with many addicted to highly concentrated Papini and Liquid Blue this proves difficult. They are not the only ones hard to assimilate back to 'normal' society, more than a thousand Space Soldiers and other personnel now reside in the moon base. Some will face trial for war crimes and the massacre of civilians, if convicted, they will serve life-terms. For President LeSouris and Colonel Kun-lee have campaigned successfully for a more humane form of justice, with capital punishment forbidden.

Former *Most Wanted* NEA-Utopian rebel and new High Priestess, Elektra Del Rey has established Utopianism as a mainstream religion, its cathedral located in the centre of Queen Elizabeth. The religion has close to half a billion adherents already, half the humans on Earth. Much to Method A's discomfort, many Jerseyans are among them after Dr VonHelmann's final sermon in New York - before the EaRA left to Mars. They pledge to make Earth greener and live a more environmentally sustainable life.

Elektra Del Rey hopes that Mars's green energy technology can be better understood and utilised on Earth next - to help regenerate it. Ensuring that not one human starves again, allowing for all to survive with decency and respect.

The clones have laid on a superb wedding feast that includes an array of once extinct crops, not grown for hundreds of years: strawberries, wheat, carrots, and lemons. So astounding that it has made headlines on Earth, which now has multiple and free broadcasting channels. Mars's green energy, bringing back much that was lost and destroyed on Earth. President Iris hopes for more progress, to bring back many of mankind's beloved animals, especially those she has read about that lived in ancient Viking settlements, lovely ginger cats, and ancient Egypt, the dotted Maus cat. But as she recited in Emily Dickinson's poem during the battle over Mars, she most of all hopes to bring back bees. If the green energy maintains a temperature over 10-degree celsius in Utopia Planitia, the bees will be able to help pollinate the flowers and make honey. Once only available from labs to cater to the tastes of the Elites, Iris dreams of a prairie with fields full of wondrous wildflowers, edible plants and bees.

The wedding reception promises some interesting entertainment, a dance and then a poetry recital from her graduating BZ clone class. With a feast that includes a dessert of delicious strawberry jam spread on bread. She's most excited about the poetry recital, it will be the first time that her class has spoken in public, having only learned to speak during the months following Dr King's death.

The clones have decided to not discuss Iris's father and his terrible deeds, but she has heard details from VanWest. The clones accept Dr VonHelmann died trying to defeat the Universal Council, to some degree atoning for his sins. They know too the Martians are not the only victims of the Council's tyranny and greed.

The wedding also marks a year since the Council's fall. Her stepsons and students still recovering mentally and physically from the bloody and unforgiving battle over Mars's skies. Together, they have built not only a new settlement but also a sense of normality and community. Iris next hopes to build a University and to invite those from Earth come to study their green planet. This green energy technology, the decorative box and mural, remains a mystery. Its source unknown - this philosopher Hans Ashtar the only link. She wants Earth's best minds to study it, but only those she can trust.

Iris walks hand-in-hand with VanWest to the dining area, lined with so many presents, including handmade products such as wrapped foods and paintings. LeSouris has cheekily gifted them part of the 'sexy' looking and now retired Hawkeye, its red eye. Barys and Kun-lee also gift more memorabilia of VanWest's adventures, having tracked down his cracked Universal Games helmet with the InsectnOut logo. But it is a present at the far end that catches VanWest's attention the most, the NASA Meatball sphere, it looks just like the one outside the Elites Quarters on the SCC-400, that too he has seen on Merritt Island, Florida in 1998.

Before he can ask who it is from, Iris whispers, 'I've saved the best present for you only'!

VanWest tries not to give away that he knows already, but he can't help himself, for he has been smiling so very happy for the last two weeks and places his hand on her belly, 'I've already named him'?

Iris giggles, 'Oh really'?

VanWest grins, 'VanWest number... no, I'm joking! I've called him Dederic after the last President of Mars'.

Iris smiles back, 'A perfect choice, my love. May we remember our past, so we don't make the same mistakes in the future'.

Iris gives VanWest another kiss as the music starts to play, the resistance song of defiance and strength, La Vie en Rose. The same song VanWest heard on the taxi's radio in 1951 Paris, on his first mission to track down the Utopians. They dance gently, awaiting the feast being laid out on the rows of white-clothed tables. Moving faster across the dance floor as the song plays louder. Iris's stepsons join in, clapping and cheering them on; the others too.

* * * * *

The light seems to be brightening. VanWest looks over at the presents once more. There are items he didn't see before, items similar in design to those he saw in Schuurman's lab. Small stone statues decorated with a face with round eyes, a crown and fangs. Others depicting a snake with feathers. The NASA Meatball sphere's shape and the name plaque is also changing, *Alpha Mission Control, Space Ken....* His hands shaking, he tries to tell Iris, but he has difficulty to articulate and find his words, 'Look! Look the sphere changes... Do you see the present'?

Iris returns a puzzled look, 'What the... The round, ancient carved stone? The name plaque reads *The Revered God Schuurman.*

Read More

VanWest
The Future

Out 2023

Book 3 in VanWest Series

Follow on Facebook and Twitter @VanWestbooks